barefoot, pajama-clad Toby asked Mitch.

"Darling, don't be rude," Abby gently scolded, putting her arm on her son's shoulder. "This is Mitch," Abby said. *Your father!* Silently she fought the almost overwhelming urge to pick up her son and run as far and as fast as her legs could carry her.

Would Mitch notice the family resemblance? Would he guess the truth? Could Toby be the reason Mitch was here? The questions buzzed like bees inside her head, and she couldn't stop the tremor of fear that vibrated through her.

Young Toby's features were almost identical to those of his father's, but neither Mitch nor Toby knew of the blood relationship they shared, and Abby...

Abby wasn't ready to reveal her secret....

Dear Reader,

Enjoy the bliss of this holiday season as six pairs of Silhouette Romance heroes and heroines discover the greatest miracle of all...true love.

Suzanne Carey warms our hearts once again with another **Fabulous Father:** *Father by Marriage*. Holly Yarborough thought her world was complete with a sweet stepdaughter until Jake McKenzie brightened their lives. But Jake was hiding something, and until Holly could convince him to trust in her love, her hope of a family with him would remain a dream.

The season comes alive in *The Merry Matchmakers* by Helen R. Myers. All Read Archer's children wanted for Christmas was a new mother. But Read didn't expect them to pick Marina Davidov, the woman who had broken his heart. Could Read give their love a second chance?

Moyra Tarling spins a tale of love renewed in *It Must Have Been the Mistletoe*. Long ago, Mitch Tyson turned Abby Roberts's world upside down. Now he was back—but could Abby risk a broken heart again and tell him the truth about her little boy?

Kate Thomas's latest work abounds with holiday cheer in *Jingle Bell Bride*. Sassy waitress Annie Patterson seemed the perfect stand-in for Matt Walker's sweet little girl. But Matt found his temporary wife's other charms even more beguiling!

And two fathers receive the greatest gift of all when they are reunited with the sons they never knew in Sally Carleen's *Cody's Christmas Wish* and *The Cowboy and the Christmas Tree* by DeAnna Talcott.

Happy Reading!

Anne Canadeo
Senior Editor

Please address questions and book requests to:
Silhouette Reader Service
U.S.: 3010 Walden Ave., P.O. Box 1325, Buffalo, NY 14269
Canadian: P.O. Box 609, Fort Erie, Ont. L2A 5X3

IT MUST HAVE BEEN THE MISTLETOE

Moyra Tarling

Silhouette
ROMANCE™
Published by Silhouette Books
America's Publisher of Contemporary Romance

To Irene,
Thanks for the love, friendship and support

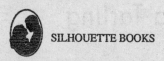

SILHOUETTE BOOKS

ISBN 0-373-19122-7

IT MUST HAVE BEEN THE MISTLETOE

Copyright © 1995 by Moyra Tarling

This edition published by arrangement with Harlequin Books S.A.

® and TM are trademarks of Harlequin Books S.A., used under
license. Trademarks indicated with ® are registered in the United States
Patent and Trademark Office, the Canadian Trade Marks Office and in
other countries.

Printed in U.S.A.

Books by Moyra Tarling

Silhouette Romance

A Tender Trail #541
A Kiss and a Promise #679
Just in Time for Christmas #763
All About Adam #782
No Mistaking Love #907
Just a Memory Away #937
Christmas Wishes #979
Finally a Family #1081
It Must Have Been the Mistletoe #1122

MOYRA TARLING

is the youngest of four children born and raised in Aberdeenshire, Scotland. It was there that she was first introduced to and became hooked on romance novels. After emigrating to Vancouver, Canada, Ms. Tarling met her future husband, Noel, at a party in Birch Bay—and promptly fell in love. They now have two children. Together they enjoy browsing through antique shops and auctions, looking for various items, from old gramophones to antique corkscrews and buttonhooks.

FIVE WAYS TO CATCH YOUR MAN UNDER THE MISTLETOE:

1—Hang mistletoe in every archway in your home so no matter where he walks, he's sure to step under some.

2—Hide mistletoe in the refrigerator and catch him during a midnight snack.

3—Tell him you need him to change a light bulb, which is conveniently located beneath the mistletoe.

4—Pretend you dropped a contact lens and are scrambling on the floor to find it. When he crouches down to help you, be sure you're under the mistletoe.

5—If all else fails, place a sprig of mistletoe in your hair and call him to the bedroom...

Chapter One

"**I**'m coming! I'm coming!" Abigail Roberts quickly dried her hands on a dish towel as she hurried to answer the doorbell's insistent summons. Dr. Stone must be doing his rounds early today, she thought as she opened the front door.

"Thanks! It's freezing out here." The man in the hooded navy parka all but shoved Abby aside in his haste to get in out of the icy December wind.

"Hey! Wait a minute!" Abby said, momentarily caught off guard. "What do you think you're doing? You can't just barge in here like that," she added, forced to retreat several steps in order to look up into the face of the newcomer.

Abby felt her heart jolt against her rib cage in startled reaction as the man tossed back the fur-trimmed hood of his parka to reveal the finely chiseled, incredibly handsome features of Mitch Tennyson.

"Mitch?" The name came out in a breathless whisper. "What are you doing here?" she managed to ask, fighting down the panic suddenly clutching at her insides. The last time she'd seen Mitch had been two years ago in Vancouver at her husband Cal's funeral. She still remembered the look of icy contempt she'd seen in the depths of Mitch's pale blue eyes when he'd stepped forward to offer his condolences.

"More to the point, what are *you* doing here?" Mitch countered, trying with difficulty to hide the shock ricocheting through him at seeing Abby, the woman whose face and body still haunted his dreams; the woman who'd saved his sanity one pain-filled night so long ago; and the woman who'd married fellow police officer Cal Roberts.

"I work for your father," Abby said, and watched Mitch's expression change to one of confusion. "I'm his nurse and housekeeper," she quickly explained.

"His nurse?" Mitch repeated, frowning in puzzlement as he unzipped his parka and removed it. The rather stilted message left on his answering machine telling him to come home hadn't said anything about his father being ill or infirm.

"Yes," Abby replied. "Your father fell and broke his hip," she told him, not surprised that Mitch didn't know about the accident. Ever since his mother's death seven years ago after a long battle with cancer, Mitch's relationship with his father had deteriorated to the point where there was little if any contact between the two men.

That had been one of the reasons she'd accepted the job as Tom Tennyson's live-in nurse and housekeeper. That and the fact that since she'd been laid off by the hospital because of budget cuts, she'd badly needed a job to help her through the approaching Christmas season.

"When did this happen?" Mitch asked, tossing his jacket on a nearby chair.

"Three weeks ago," Abby replied, trying to ignore the way her pulse was tripping over at the sight of his lean, muscular frame, dressed in a bright checkered shirt and hip-hugging blue jeans.

"Why wasn't I notified?" Mitch asked, anger evident in his tone, forgetting for a moment that he'd been working undercover in Toronto for the past month, trying to break up a counterfeit ring.

"You'll have to ask Dr. Stone," she said, tempted for a moment to tell Mitch that his father had been the one who'd vetoed the doctor's suggestion to contact Mitch.

"How did it happen?" Mitch asked.

"He fell off a ladder at the store," she explained.

Mitch's father owned and operated Tennyson's Market, located on Peachville's main street. Tennyson's was something of a landmark, having the honor of being one of the first stores built in town.

"What the hell was he doing up a ladder in the first place?" Mitch wanted to know. "Doesn't he have employees to do that for him?" He ran a hand through his dark hair, creating a disheveled appearance that merely served to enhance his good looks. "Was it a bad break?" His eyes lifted once more to meet hers.

Abby disregarded the shiver of awareness that shimmied up her spine as he held her gaze. "Pretty bad," she said. "The orthopedic surgeon, Dr. Franz, recommended a complete hip replacement. Your father came through the operation with flying colors," she quickly assured him, refraining from adding that since being discharged from the hospital a little over a week ago, Tom had refused to follow doctor's orders and appeared totally uninterested in getting back on his feet.

"Shouldn't he be in the hospital?" Mitch asked. "No...forget it," he hurried on. "Ever since my mother's illness was diagnosed, Dad developed a hatred for hospitals." It was sentiment Mitch understood well, considering that only two days ago he'd checked himself out of a hospital in Toronto. "I suppose the only way the doctors would have gotten him to stay would have been to keep him under sedation or tie him down," he went on.

"Exactly," Abby replied. "That's why I'm here. Dr. Stone threatened to keep your father in the hospital indefinitely unless he hired someone to look after him."

"I see," Mitch said, but before he could comment further a sound at the top of the stairs had them both turning in that direction.

"Mom? I heard voices. Oh... Who are you?" A barefoot young boy, wearing pajamas decorated with a multi-

tude of cartoon characters, came down the stairs toward
them.

"Darling, don't be rude," Abby scolded as the child
reached the tiled entranceway and came to a halt at her side.
Putting her arm on her son's shoulder, Abby threw an
anxious glance at Mitch, who was staring at the boy with
obvious interest.

Her heart picked up speed and apprehension danced
down her spine when she saw a faint frown appear on
Mitch's face. Silently she fought the almost overwhelming
urge to pick up her son and run as far and as fast as her legs
could carry her.

Would Mitch notice the family resemblance? Would he
guess the truth? Could Toby be the reason Mitch was here?
The questions buzzed like bees inside her head, and she
couldn't stop the tremor of fear that vibrated through her.

Young Toby's features were almost identical to those of
his father's, but neither Mitch nor Toby knew of the blood
relationship they shared, and Abby had no intention of ever
revealing her secret. The only person who had known the
truth about Toby's parentage had been her husband, Cal,
killed two years ago in the line of duty while attempting to
apprehend an armed robber.

"You must be Toby," Mitch said, his tone warm, his
smile friendly.

Toby glanced nervously up at his mother, then back at
Mitch. "How'd you know my name?" the boy asked,
nudging closer to Abby.

"I knew Cal . . . I knew your father," Mitch amended,
noting instantly the shuttered look that came into the boy's
eyes before he buried his face in his mother's apron.

"He's a bit shy," Abby explained. Gently she stroked her
son's dark hair. "Sweetheart," she said softly, "this is
Mitch. He's Mr. Tennyson's son," she explained, and at her
words she felt his hold on her slowly relax. She glanced
once more at Mitch, intent on distracting his attention away
from Toby. "I was just going to take your father his
breakfast tray," she said. "Maybe you'd like to take it up
for him? It might help break the ice."

"Sure," said Mitch after a brief hesitation. Not having seen his father in five years, Mitch wasn't sure what kind of reception he would get, but there seemed little point in delaying the meeting.

The woman's voice on his answering machine telling him his father needed him had been vaguely familiar but not one he'd readily recognized.

But the call had been timely indeed and precisely the excuse he'd needed to make the journey home. Home! He'd been thinking about home and his father rather a lot lately, due in part, he knew, to the incident that had resulted in his own brief hospital stay.

Besides, with Christmas only three weeks away, what better time to try to make peace with his father? He only hoped it wasn't too late, that the gap between them hadn't widened to a chasm.

"I just finished putting his tray together," Abby said. "The coffee will have cooled off by now. And there's nothing your father hates more than cold coffee. I'd better pour him a fresh cup," she added as she gently urged Toby toward the kitchen, all the while aware of the man following close behind.

Toby ran on ahead and scrambled onto one of the kitchen chairs. Abby crossed to the counter where she'd left Tom's breakfast tray. Dumping the lukewarm coffee into the sink, she refilled the cup from the carafe on the counter.

"There you are," she said, holding out the tray.

"Is this all he eats?" Mitch asked, scanning the halved grapefruit and two slices of toast on the tray, a far cry from the hearty breakfasts his mother had always made for him and his father.

"He doesn't have his appetite back yet," she told him, wanting to prepare Mitch for the change he would undoubtedly see in the older man.

As he took the tray from her, his fingers briefly brushed hers, and at the contact a quicksilver tingle of sensation raced up her arm, startling her. Her eyes flew to meet his and for a heart-stopping second an emotion she couldn't decipher flashed in the depths of his pale blue eyes.

With her heart beating an unsteady rhythm against her breastbone, Abby turned away and, picking up the sponge on the counter, began to wipe a sink that was already clean. When she ventured to glance around a few moments later she was relieved to see that he'd gone.

Abby slowly released the breath she'd been holding, silently chastising herself for not being able to control her reaction to Mitch. But that was a skill she'd never quite mastered, not since the first time she'd set eyes on him—the summer she'd turned sixteen when he'd come home to Peachville to spend the vacation with his parents before starting work as a police officer with the Vancouver Police Department.

At that time Abby had been enjoying her summer job as a cashier at Tennyson's Market. She could still recall quite vividly the day Mitch had popped in to see his father, and to say hello to everyone at the store.

Dressed in jean cutoffs and a white muscle shirt that accentuated the breadth of his powerful shoulders, Mitch had looked utterly devastating, and the friendly smile he'd thrown her way had quite simply been her undoing, sending her heart into a tailspin.

There had been something about him, something primitive, something indefinably male, that had set him apart from all the adolescent boys she knew at school. In that split second she'd fallen head over heels in love, a feeling that hadn't diminished with either time or distance.

Several years later, when she'd been accepted into the nurses' program at the University of British Columbia in Vancouver, she'd fantasized about one day running into Mitch Tennyson. But never in her wildest dreams would she have envisioned that meeting him again would set in motion a series of events that would affect her life so profoundly.

"Mom, can I have some of that apple-cinnamon-flavored oatmeal?" Toby's question penetrated the thick fog of her memories, effectively bringing her out of the haze.

"Of course you can," Abby replied cheerfully as she reached for the package of cereal.

"Mom, it's snowing again," Toby said excitedly. "Do you really think we'll have a white Christmas?"

"It's definitely beginning to look that way," Abby said as she glanced outside at the large flakes drifting past the kitchen window.

It had been snowing intermittently for the past three days and the landscape had taken on a pristine appearance, much like a scene from a Christmas card. Her prediction that there would be snow on the ground for Christmas had been based on those Christmases she'd spent in Peachville.

The five years she and her mother had lived in Peachville had been the longest they'd stayed anywhere, and Abby had grown to love the small town where she'd spent some of the happiest times of her life.

That's why she'd decided to come back. She'd wanted to give Toby the chance to experience the same kind of happiness, to live in a place where family values were strong and community spirit played a big part in everyone's life. She'd wanted her son to build memories of his own—happy memories. And she was determined that Toby's first Christmas in Peachville would be his best Christmas ever.

"I hope the school bus doesn't get stuck in the snow," Toby said, a hint of anxiety in his voice. "Mrs. Spracklin wants to run through the Christmas play this afternoon, and we're all supposed to have memorized our lines."

Abby smiled. Ever since Toby had been chosen to play the part of one of the three wise men, he'd talked of little else. "Don't worry, the bus always gets through," she assured him.

Since taking up residence in Tom Tennyson's rambling old house four miles out of Peachville a little over a week ago, Toby had been traveling to and from the elementary school in town on the big orange school bus that stopped at the end of the driveway.

The bus ride had quickly become a highlight of her son's day, and Abby still marveled at the transformation that had taken place in Toby ever since they'd made the move to Peachville.

When school started he'd made friends with the other children in his first-grade class, several of whom rode the bus with him each day. And slowly but surely she'd watched his confidence grow until he'd broken free of the protective shell he'd built around himself, confirming that Abby's decision to build a new life in the place where she'd once known happiness herself had indeed been the right one.

And while Mitch's arrival was both unexpected and unforeseen, there was little she could do but hope that his visit would be a short one, that he was just passing through.

Seven years ago on a rainy night in Vancouver, a night she'd never forgotten, a night she'd never regretted, they'd shared a passion that had touched her soul. And Toby, the child she loved as much as she'd once loved the man who'd fathered him, had been the result of that unparalleled encounter. But Mitch had walked out of her life without as much as a backward glance, leaving Abby to deal with the consequences of that night on her own.

The sound of approaching footsteps cut through Abby's musings, and inwardly she braced herself for his return.

"Well, that was an unmitigated disaster," Mitch said as he reentered the kitchen. Crossing to the coffee carafe, he helped himself to a mug from the stand on the counter and filled it.

"I gather it wasn't a happy reunion," Abby said.

"How did you guess?" Mitch responded, sarcasm evident in his tone. "He's still the same stubborn old—" He broke off, suddenly remembering there was a child in the room.

After pulling out one of the remaining three chairs he sat opposite Toby, who was studying him with interest.

"Doesn't Mr. Tom like you?" Toby asked him.

"You got that right," Mitch replied with a sigh as he sipped thoughtfully on his coffee. While he hadn't exactly expected to be greeted with open arms, he had hoped his father might give some small indication that he was glad to see him. But there had been no glimmer of warmth in his eyes, no welcoming smile from the man lying on the bed. But what disturbed Mitch most was the change in the older man's appearance. Always a robust, healthy man, his father now looked smaller, older and strangely fragile.

"You have to remember that your father's been through quite a lot these past few weeks," Abby said in an attempt to ease the frustration she could see etched on Mitch's handsome features.

Mitch sighed and nodded. "I suppose you're right," he said, surprised how much he'd needed to hear her words of comfort, yet at the same time wondering why facing criminals and thugs seemed so much easier than dealing with his father.

Up until the time his mother had become ill his relationship with his father—with both his parents, for that matter—had been a close one. But when the doctors had informed them that the cancer was untreatable, all of their lives had changed dramatically.

His father had received the news with anger, shock and dismay. Mitch, on the other hand, had been devastated, too stunned to even react, and in his anguish and despair his father had interpreted Mitch's lack of reaction as being that of a cold and uncaring son. And so instead of the mutual pain and grief drawing them together, it had torn them apart.

"Why doesn't Mr. Tom like you?" Toby asked, effectively bringing Mitch's attention back to the boy.

"Toby..." Abby cautioned, frowning at her son. "It's not polite to ask personal questions."

"That's all right," Mitch said easily.

"Did you do something wrong?" Toby persisted, obviously finding the topic intriguing.

"My father thinks so," Mitch replied, recalling how his father had made no bones about showing his disapproval whenever Mitch stepped out of line. Not for the first time he found himself wondering if he was wasting his time, that trying to make peace with his father wasn't simply a lost cause.

"My father didn't..." Toby began.

"Toby!" Abby quickly jumped in. "The school bus will be here shortly. You'd better hurry upstairs and get dressed," she said, managing to keep her tone even. Her heart, however, was hammering at an alarming rate. "Would you like a peanut butter and jelly sandwich for lunch today?'' she asked, her aim simply to distract her son's attention further, positive that Toby had been about to say that his father ''didn't like me, either,'' a fact and feeling Cal had never bothered to hide.

''Yes, please,'' Toby responded before licking his spoon clean. ''May I be excused?'' he asked.

''Yes, and don't forget to brush your teeth,'' Abby called as Toby hopped down from the chair and dashed from the kitchen. Relieved that she'd managed to avert a potential disaster, Abby turned to Mitch. ''Would you like some breakfast?''

''I'll get it. I don't expect you to wait on me,'' he added, starting to rise from his chair.

''No! Sit down! It's no problem,'' she quickly countered, wanting to avoid at all costs any close contact with him. ''Is instant oatmeal all right?''

''What other kind is there?'' he replied as he sank back onto the chair, puzzled by what he perceived as her nervousness, and curious to know why Abby had cut Toby off so abruptly.

Slowly Mitch let his gaze roam over Abby as she reached for a bowl from the stack in the cupboard. Her hips, he noted, were fuller now and the curve of her breasts more voluptuous. Suddenly a need strong and intense gripped him, taking him by surprise and making him long to explore those new and alluring contours, to taste again the delicious secrets of her body, and reawaken the passion that had ignited with such startling ferocity that night seven years ago... when she'd brought him back from the brink of despair.

She'd been his savior, his sanctuary, as well as his lover that night, and he'd never been able to forget the depth of passion they'd shared. But it had been two long months before he'd seen her again, only to be greeted with the stunning news that she was marrying Cal, a fellow police officer.

''Here you are,'' Abby said as she set the bowl of steaming oatmeal in front of him.

"Thanks," he replied, managing with some difficulty to bring his thoughts under control, annoyed that the memory still had the power to affect him.

Abby nodded in acknowledgment before moving away to retrieve Toby's lunch box from the cupboard near the sink.

"How old is Toby now?" Mitch asked.

Abby felt her breath lock in her throat at the question. "Ah...he's six," she said after what seemed a lengthy pause, fearful that Mitch might ask the date of Toby's birth.

"Six," Mitch repeated. "So he was four when Cal died. Old enough to have some memories of his father."

Abby almost dropped the knife she'd taken from the cutlery drawer. For the second time in as many minutes, her heart began to race out of control.

"A few," she answered carefully, silently reminding herself to remain calm. Mitch was a policeman, trained in the art of observation, skilled at spotting a lie. Taking a deep, steadying breath, Abby focused her attention on spreading peanut butter on the bread.

"Cal was quite a cop," Mitch said, managing to keep the sarcasm out of his voice. He and Cal had attended basic training together, but there had been no love lost between them.

Abby felt the blood drain from her face at Mitch's words, and all at once the sour taste of bile rose in her mouth.

"Is my lunch ready, Mom?" Toby's question effectively cut through a silence that was decidedly tense.

"Almost," Abby managed to say, glad of the interruption, which provided her with a few moments' respite and an excuse not to answer Mitch's comment.

With practiced ease she finished making the sandwich and deftly wrapped it in wax paper. After gathering together a banana, an apple and a container of juice, she put everything into her son's lunch box. "Get your jacket and boots on, and I'll walk you to the bus," she said after glancing at the digital clock on the microwave.

"Oh...I almost forgot," Toby said. "Mr. Tom said he wants to see you, Mom."

"I'll walk Toby to the bus, if you like," Mitch offered before Abby could reply.

"No!" Abby said quickly, too quickly, because Mitch was frowning at her now. "Thanks, Mitch, but it's really not necessary," she said, keeping her tone even. "Toby can easily walk down the driveway to the bus on his own."

"It's really no problem," Mitch countered. "Besides, I'm curious to know who's driving the school bus these days," he added.

"Mrs. MacGillicuddy is our bus driver," Toby said, pronouncing the name carefully. "We call her Mrs. Mac," he added.

Mitch smiled at this news. "Well, that settles it. I'll have to walk you to the bus," he said. "Because if Vera finds out that the truck in the driveway is mine, she'll never forgive me if I don't go and say hello."

Abby had little choice but to smile and accept his offer. Any further protest would surely result in arousing Mitch's curiosity. She followed Toby to the foyer, where she helped him with his jacket and boots.

"Come on, sport." Mitch stood at the open door wearing his parka. "Last one to the bus stop is a rotten egg."

Toby grinned up at Mitch, and Abby felt her heart constrict with pain at the look of surprise and pleasure that had appeared on her son's face in response to Mitch's playful challenge. Cal, the man everyone assumed was Toby's father, had ignored the child from the moment she'd brought him home from the hospital, and Abby had never forgiven herself for allowing Cal to manipulate her into a marriage that hadn't been a marriage at all.

"Bye, Mom!" Toby called, and clutching his lunch box he ran past Mitch into the snow.

"Bye!" Abby gazed after the twosome, her vision blurred by the tears gathering in her eyes. What she had just witnessed was exactly the kind of exchange that should occur between a father and his son.

And that's all she'd ever wanted for her child. A father, a man who would guide and mold her son into a strong, decent and loving human being. She wanted what every

child should have and what she herself had never known—
the love of a father.

Her father had left before she was born. Abby had spent
her childhood hoping and dreaming that one day he would
appear and tell her how much he loved her. Instead, those
early years had been spent moving from place to place with
her mother, never putting down roots. She'd hated the no-
madic existence and vowed that her baby would be brought
up in a stable environment with two loving parents.

But marrying Cal had been a mistake, the biggest mistake she'd ever made. A mistake all the harder to bear because, painful as it had been for her, Toby had suffered
more, and Abby blamed herself.

She'd soon discovered that beneath the charming facade
Cal showed to the outside world lay a troubled man, a
jealous man, a man obsessed. But he'd shown her only the
side he'd wanted her to see, cleverly manipulating her by
playing on her fears and insecurities at a time when she'd
been at her most vulnerable.

A shiver chased down Abby's spine as these memories
flitted across her mind. Annoyed with herself and the route
her thoughts had taken, she brushed the moisture from her
eyes and pushed all thoughts of Cal aside.

Closing the door against the bone-chilling December
wind, she reminded herself that Cal no longer had the
power to hurt her. The past, or at least part of it, was behind her now. She'd fought hard to make a new and better
life for herself and Toby here in Peachville, and she wasn't
about to let anything or anyone destroy the happiness and
peace of mind they'd both found.

With a sigh, Abby headed for the stairs. Tom would be
wondering what had become of her, and she was suddenly
curious what, if anything, he had to say about Mitch's unexpected appearance.

Hurrying along the landing, she tapped lightly on the
open door and went inside.

"It's about time," Tom said gruffly, looking up at her
from the bed.

"And a good morning to you, too," Abby countered
with a smile, ignoring his comment. She crossed to the bed

and removed the tray, noting with some satisfaction that he'd eaten everything. "Would you like more coffee?"

"Yes, thank you, I would," Tom replied. "Ah . . . is he still here?" he asked tentatively.

"Who?" Abby replied, knowing full well that Tom was talking about Mitch, but seeing also that for the first time since the ambulance attendants had carried Tom Tennyson to his room and helped him into bed, there was a spark of interest shining in the depths of the old man's eyes.

"Don't play games with me, young lady," Tom grumbled, though there was no real anger in his tone. "You know exactly who I'm talking about. Mitch. Is he still here?" He repeated the question and Abby heard the hint of anxiety beneath the gruff manner.

"Yes. He's still here," Abby said, setting the tray on the dressing table nearby.

"Did he say how long he planned to stay?" Tom asked, his fingers curling at the bed covers in anticipation of her answer.

It was a question she wouldn't have minded knowing the answer to herself, Abby thought as she leaned over to fluff up his pillows and straighten the bedclothes. "No, he didn't say," she answered.

"Humph..." her patient responded. "I haven't seen hide nor hair of him in five years and then he walks in large as life and twice as cocky. Don't suppose he's doing anything other than passing through on his way to his detective's job with the Vancouver police," he complained, bitterness seeping into his voice now. "All he cares about is catching crooks. And if you ask me that's a colossal waste of time, because they're back on the streets before you can say 'Bob's your uncle.' What's the good of that?"

Abby made no reply, all the while thinking that since she and Toby had moved into the house she'd never seen him so animated or so agitated about anything. Mitch's appearance had given Tom a much-needed jolt in the arm, and Abby could only hope that it signaled an end to the depression that had been hanging over Tom ever since his release from the hospital.

Suddenly the sound of voices and footfalls in the hall-way caught their attention and Abby turned to see Mitch, accompanied by one of Peachville's best-loved doctors, Robert Stone.

"Good morning, Tom. Look who I found wandering around outside in the snow." Bob Stone smiled at Mitch. "He's looking a bit pale and thin, don't you think? Probably all that city living," he teased as he gave Mitch a friendly slap on the back. Dr. Stone crossed to the bed and set his black bag on top of the quilt. "I was telling Mitch you're coming along fine and that you'll soon be up and about again, with the help of a walker, of course."

"I've told you before, I like it fine right here," Tom said, scowling at his friend.

"That's the whole problem. You like it too much," the doctor was quick to respond. "But the rest is doing you good. Your blood pressure has come down."

"Blood pressure?" Mitch queried.

"Your father's had a problem for a year or two now," Dr. Stone said. "I've told him it's the stress of running the store. He forgets he's not as young as he once was, that he can't do everything himself. It's high time he thought about retiring, but he won't listen to me. He's a stubborn old cuss," the doctor commented dryly.

"Retire! Pah! If I retire, the store would close within six months," came the indignant reply.

Dr. Stone shook his head. "See what I mean?" He shrugged. "I hope you're planning to stick around for a while, Mitch, because it's time someone made your father see sense."

Mitch smiled ruefully. "And what makes you think he'll listen to me?" he responded.

"You won't be staying long enough to make no never mind," Tom muttered somewhat caustically under his breath.

Mitch bristled at his father's comment. "Well, I'm sorry to have to disappoint you, Dad," he said.

"Disappoint me? What do you mean?" Tom gazed up at his son.

Abby caught the glimmer of hope that sprang into Tom's eyes at Mitch's remark and felt her own pulse pick up speed as she waited, with a mixture of anticipation and dread, for his answer.

"I'm not going back to Vancouver—at least, not yet," Mitch stated evenly, and Abby felt her heart shudder to a halt then kick into overdrive.

"What do you mean, you're not going back to Vancouver?" Tom's expression was one of disbelief. "What about your job?" he asked.

"Oh...I guess in all the excitement of my arrival I forgot to mention that I'm on a leave of absence from work. You're stuck with me for a while...at least until the New Year," Mitch said with a smile.

Chapter Two

"Well, that's what I call good timing," said Dr. Stone, who was the first to respond to Mitch's startling announcement.

"I'm glad you think so, Doc," Mitch said, but it was his father's reaction that interested him more, and he quickly flicked his glance back to the man in the bed. A look of surprise as well as another emotion—was it relief?—flashed briefly in the older man's eyes before it was replaced with a familiar scowl.

Lifting his gaze once more, Mitch was in time to see the expression of dismay that appeared on Abby's face before she quickly schooled her features. He frowned, at a loss to understand Abby's reaction. That she should care one way or the other seemed strange, but, on reflection, he realized that from the moment she'd opened the door for him earlier he'd detected a tension in her, a nervousness that puzzled him.

Abby curled her hands into fists in an attempt to hide the fact that they were shaking. Aware that Mitch was watching her, she pinned a smile on her face, ignoring the pain beginning to throb insistently at her temples.

Keeping her smile in place, she turned to pick up the tray. "Please excuse me. I have work to do," she said and, without waiting for a reply, made her way from the bedroom.

With her heart still drumming a frantic beat, Abby reached the relative sanctuary of the kitchen. Setting the tray next to the sink, she leaned heavily against the counter and clamped her hand against her mouth to stem the moan threatening to erupt.

Mitch was staying! He was staying! The words played like a litany inside her head and she felt her whole body begin to tremble like a leaf in a windstorm. Just when she'd begun to put her life back together, just when the future for herself and her son had taken a turn for the better, fate had tossed a new player into the game. Mitch.

Resolutely Abby tried to convince herself she had nothing to fear, that Mitch had no inkling whatsoever Toby was *his* son. But, not for the first time since learning of her pregnancy, Abby wondered what Mitch's response would be if he ever found out the truth.

He wouldn't find out! He couldn't. Besides, she doubted he would believe her. Cal had seen to that.

As reason slowly returned, Abby felt the panic inside her begin to abate. She was overreacting, that was all. Mitch's sudden reappearance had stirred up old memories, memories she'd buried in a secret corner of her heart, memories she would do well to forget altogether.

But she'd never quite been able to banish Mitch from her mind. How could she? When every day she was reminded of him by simply gazing into the face of their son. But how long would it be before Mitch began to notice the resemblance? How long before someone, Tom perhaps, would make a comment that Toby looked a lot like Mitch, or vice versa?

What she had to do was keep Toby away from Mitch as much as possible and hope that he wouldn't make the damaging connection. And as for herself, she would have to maintain a professional distance and do her utmost to control her body's errant reactions whenever Mitch was near.

"Is there any coffee left?" Mitch asked as he joined her in the kitchen.

Abby jumped at the sound of his voice, and immediately her pulse began to behave erratically. "Ah...yes," she said, keeping her back to him, annoyed at how quickly her resolve had failed her, and furious at her inability to control her response. "Help yourself." She started to wash the dishes, gritting her teeth in frustration as she silently willed her speeding heart to slow down.

"It's not for me. It's for my father. He wants another cup," Mitch replied, taking a step toward her.

"Oh...right, I completely forgot," Abby said, knowing the reason for her distraction had been her preoccupation with Mitch and the news that he was staying. Shaking the dishwater from her hands, she turned to grab the towel she'd tossed over the back of the kitchen chair, only to collide with Mitch's solid frame.

At the contact her breath froze in her lungs and her heart, already beating in double time, began to flutter against her breast like a panicked bird fighting for its freedom. Mesmerized by the sight of her wet hands splayed across the front of his shirt, Abby felt a bolt of heat race through her, almost as if she'd touched a live wire.

Beneath her fingers she could feel the steady rhythm of his heart, and she found herself remembering all too clearly the last time he'd held her like this. She lifted her gaze to meet his, hoping for one foolish moment he might remember, too, but except for the flicker of emotion that briefly clouded his pale eyes, his expression remained controlled and decidedly unreadable.

All at once his hands came up to grip her upper arms. Slowly he eased her body away from his. But he didn't let go. Through the thickness of her sweater his touch seemed to sear her and every nerve reacted in unison, igniting a need she'd all but forgotten, reawakening a desire more powerful than she remembered.

Her legs felt like two strands of wet spaghetti and threatened to give way under her as she tried to cope with the barrage of sensations assailing her. Her heart skidded to a halt before gathering speed once more as Mitch slowly, tantalizingly began to close the gap between them. A tell-tale tremor danced across her nerve endings and her eyelids fluttered closed in heady anticipation of his mouth claiming hers.

The shrill ring of the telephone cut through the silence, and they jumped apart like two guilty teenagers caught in a compromising position. Abby, a raging torrent of unfulfilled longings, somehow managed to move away from Mitch toward the instrument hanging on the wall next to the fridge.

"Hello." She spoke into the receiver, surprised that her voice sounded normal when her entire body vibrated like the strings of a newly played guitar.

"Abby, this is Joyce Alexander." The caller introduced herself. "How are you this morning?"

"I'm fine, Mrs. Alexander," Abby lied, fighting to hear her over the thundering roar of her heartbeat. "How are you?" she asked politely. Joyce Alexander was a friend and contemporary of Tom Tennyson and lived in nearby Meadowvale.

"Fine, dear, thank you," came the reply. "Listen, Abby, I just had a call from Vera MacGillicuddy," Joyce went on. "She told me she spoke to Mitch this morning. Is it true? Has he come home?"

"Yes...yes, he has," Abby confirmed, thinking that Vera hadn't wasted any time in passing along the news of Mitch's return. "He's right here. Would you like to speak to him?"

"Oh ... Why, yes ... thank you, I would," Joyce said.

"Hold on," Abby said, then covered the mouthpiece as she turned to Mitch. "It's Joyce Alexander. She wants to talk to you."

Mitch stared blankly at her for a moment. "Joyce Alexander." He repeated the name, and suddenly he realized that Joyce, one of his mother's dearest friends, had been the person responsible for leaving the message on his answering machine. "Oh ... yes, of course," he said, crossing to where Abby stood.

Abby felt her heart kick against her rib cage in alarm and she hastily held out the receiver, intent on avoiding any further physical contact with Mitch. As Mitch took the telephone from her, their fingers made fleeting contact, and it was all Abby could do not to snatch her hand away.

"Hello, Joyce. How are you?" Abby barely heard Mitch's polite question as she crossed to the kitchen sink. With hands that weren't quite steady she poured coffee into a mug.

"Thank you. Yes, I did," Mitch said as Abby, mug in hand, made her escape.

As she climbed the stairs, the thought of what had almost happened sent a shiver of renewed awareness chasing down her spine. Her whole body—every cell, every nerve—still ached with the need his nearness had aroused. She could scarcely bear to think what would have happened had he kissed her.

Angrily she reminded herself that she was a mature woman of twenty-nine now and not the naive young innocent she'd been seven years ago when she'd let her heart rule her head and surrendered to the desire he'd ignited with one devastating kiss.

That she'd been in love with Mitch from the first moment she set eyes on him had been the only excuse, and a poor one at that, for her wanton behavior that night so long ago. She'd allowed her emotions to cloud her judgment, and not for the first time she acknowledged that she'd been a prize fool to think that just because Mitch had made love to her, he must also be *in love* with her.

It was a distinction she'd quickly come to recognize, and a differentiation that had been painfully brought home to her when he'd vanished from her bed in the early hours of the morning without even saying goodbye.

But she wasn't the first, nor would she be the last, woman to have her adolescent dreams and youthful fantasies shattered by a man. The trick was not to make the same mistake twice.

"Ah... there's my coffee." Tom greeted her with a hint of a smile as she tapped on the bedroom door and entered. "Doc, do you have time to join me for a cup this morning?"

"Thank you for the offer, but I'd better be on my way," said the doctor, snapping his black bag closed. "I'll see you tomorrow. Weather permitting, that is," he continued. "I heard on the radio that there's a storm heading this way. The announcer predicted there would be a foot or more of snow before midnight."

Tom scoffed. "Those weather folks are wrong more often than they're right," he said derisively. "The way my bunion's been aching lately, I'd say we're likely to get a darned sight more than a foot of snow, closer to three."

The doctor laughed. "Of course, your bunion is much more reliable than all the sophisticated weather equipment they have nowadays," he teased.

"Laugh if you like, but my bunion's never been wrong yet," Tom countered.

"If that's the case, then you won't be seeing me for a couple of days," he said. "Take care," he added as he followed Abby from the room.

"If Tom and the weathermen are right and a storm is due, you'll be stranded here for a day or two until the plow gets through. It's a good thing Mitch showed up when he did. You'd have a tough time digging yourself out of the driveway," the doctor commented when they reached the bottom of the stairs.

"I'm not sure Tom would agree with you—about Mitch, I mean," Abby said, refraining from adding that she was even less enthusiastic than her patient at the thought of having Mitch around.

"Much as he might protest, I think deep down Tom's happy to have his son home," said Dr. Stone as he pulled on his wool jacket. "Besides, it's high time those two settled their differences. Rose would be appalled if she knew they've been carrying on all these years like a pair of quarrelsome children." He shook his head. "Mitch's arrival has already had a positive effect. It's shaken Tom out of the depression he's been wallowing in. His hip is healing nicely. The next step is to get him up and mobile again."

"Other than putting a stick of dynamite under him, what would you suggest?" The question came from Mitch, who'd appeared from the direction of the kitchen.

Abby kept her attention on the doctor, ignoring the quick leap her heart took at the sound of Mitch's voice.

"To tell you the truth, I don't know," the doctor replied with a rueful smile. "That's your problem," he added just as the grandfather clock in the hall began to chime out the hour. "Look at the time. If I want to get the rest of my rounds done, I'd better get going."

"I'll walk you to your car," Mitch said, and followed the doctor out into the snow.

Leaving the door ajar, Abby returned to the kitchen, wondering all the while just how she was going to get through the next few weeks living under the same roof with Mitch.

Her thoughts shifted to Dr. Stone's conversation about the weather. If a storm was heading their way, she would need to stock up on grocery items. When she'd first arrived at the house, it had come as no surprise to discover that Tom had been living somewhat of a bachelor's existence, with both refrigerator and food cupboards almost empty.

She'd spent her second day on the job restoring order and cleanliness to the kitchen. After giving all the counters a good scrubbing, she'd made a list of the food items she'd needed and driven into town to Tennyson's Market to stock up. Those supplies were now running low, and with Mitch's arrival and the approaching storm she knew she would be wise to pay a visit to the market.

"Abby..." Mitch's voice cut through her thoughts and she turned to find him standing in the doorway. "Which bedrooms are you and Toby using?"

"My room is the one at the end of the hall. Toby's is right next door," she told him.

"Good. That means I can use my old room," he said and turned to go.

"It's all aired out," she replied, having spent several days cleaning the bedrooms on the upper floor. "You'll find clean sheets in the linen closet."

That the house had been badly neglected since the death of Rose Tennyson had been painfully obvious, but over the past week Abby had managed to restore order to most of the rooms once cared for and loved by Tom's wife.

It hadn't been difficult to figure out which room belonged to Mitch—she'd known by the array of football trophies displayed on his dresser. At first she'd been reluctant to enter his room, fearful that if she crossed the threshold she might discover more about Mitch than she wanted to know. But after overcoming her initial aversion, she'd found that there had been little in the room, other than the trophies, to indicate that Mitch had once been its occupant.

"Great," Mitch said. "I'll take care of that right now. Oh, by the way, I thought I'd drive to the gas station in town and have chains put on my truck. Is there anything you need?"

Abby felt her heart skip a beat at the question. "I needed you seven years ago!" she wanted to shout, but she bit back the words, swallowing to alleviate the sudden dryness in her throat.

"Are you going to drop in at your father's store?" she asked a moment later.

"Probably. Why?" he asked.

"I haven't been into town this week to grocery shop," she said. "If that storm Dr. Stone was talking about hits here, we're going to run short of supplies. The problem is my list is rather long."

Mitch frowned. When he'd made the offer he'd been thinking along the lines of picking up a gallon of milk or a loaf of bread, but from what Abby had just said she needed much more than a few basics. "Maybe it would be easier if you came with me," he said.

"No...really, that's all right." Abby was quick to decline his offer. The thought of being stuck in the confines of a vehicle with Mitch for any length of time had little appeal, and was a situation to be avoided if at all possible. "I have my own car. I'll drive in later," she added and at her words saw his dark eyebrows rise in silent query.

"I don't see the point of taking two vehicles," he said.

"I don't want to slow you down," she replied, knowing her excuse was lame.

"I'm not leaving right now," he assured her. "Besides, if you wait, you run the risk of getting caught in the storm," he noted.

"My car has snow tires," Abby said, wishing now she'd said no to his initial offer. She could see by the tightening of his jaw that he was becoming annoyed.

"And my truck is really Santa's sleigh," Mitch countered. "Come on, Abby, what's the problem here?" he asked, frustration putting an edge to his tone. He couldn't quite figure out why she seemed reluctant to make the journey into town with him. She was nervous, that much was obvious, but why?

All at once those moments when he'd collided with her in the kitchen leapt into his mind. She'd felt it, too, the awareness that had arced between them. If the telephone hadn't rung, would he have kissed her? It wasn't a question he was ready to answer.

Seven years ago, on the night of his mother's death, he'd found solace in Abby's arms, believing she was an angel sent to comfort him in his hour of need. But later, when he'd learned that on the night he'd made love to her she'd been practically engaged to marry another man, the knowledge had shattered him.

He'd thought something special had happened between them that night, something lasting, only to realize that she'd merely taken pity on him and the passion they'd shared had meant nothing to her.

Amid the disgust and anger he'd felt was a sense of betrayal. He'd trusted his heart to her that night, only to have her trample it underfoot, and he'd vowed never to make the same mistake again.

"I suppose you're right. Taking two vehicles isn't exactly practical." Abby's voice cut through Mitch's wayward thoughts, bringing his attention back to the present. "When are you planning on leaving?" she asked.

"Can you be ready in twenty minutes?"

"No problem," she replied.

It was in fact half an hour later before they made their way out to Mitch's truck. In that time Abby had fixed Tom a small thermos of hot chocolate and a sandwich, to eat while they were gone.

Mitch was silent as he started the engine and headed the truck down the driveway. As Abby huddled for warmth inside her olive green winter coat, she gazed out at the gray clouds gathering in a sky filled with the promise of snow and wondered if the storm was moving in faster than had been predicted.

Snowflakes, like tiny white insects, sailed intermittently past the windshield while the wipers swatted at them ineffectually. Mitch reached over and switched on the truck's heater and soon warm air was blasting at them, chasing away the winter chill.

When the truck made the turn onto the road leading toward town, Abby glanced at Mitch's profile and felt her heart give a familiar little leap. Seven years ago, lying beside him watching him as he slept, she'd memorized every last feature, from the neatly trimmed jet black hair that fell across his forehead in inviting disarray to the tiny dimple in the center of his chin that matched young Toby's to a T.

Mitch's lovemaking that night had been intense, inspired and incredibly exciting, taking her to heights she'd only ever thought existed within the pages of a romance novel.

But unlike the characters in those novels, whose story always ended happily, their ending had been a far cry from "happily ever after." She'd been brought painfully back to reality when, after drifting off to sleep herself, she'd awakened in the early hours of the morning to discover that Mitch had crept away like a phantom in the night without as much as a kiss goodbye.

She'd waited expectantly for the phone to ring. But when the hours had turned into days and then weeks without a word from Mitch, her hopes and dreams had begun to unravel, leaving her nowhere to go and no one to turn to except Cal.

"Tell me, what made you move back to Peachville?" Mitch's question effectively cut into her reverie. "I would have thought you'd stay in Vancouver to be near Cal's family," he went on. "His father still lives there, doesn't he?"

Abby was surprised Mitch knew so much about Cal's family. Though Cal had worked out of the same police headquarters as Mitch, Cal had told her he didn't know Mitch very well.

"Cal's father remarried last year," Abby told him. "His new wife's from Australia. They decided to set up house over there."

"That's too bad. Toby won't have any grandparents around to spoil him," Mitch commented, throwing her a sideways glance.

"Mmm..." Abby responded noncommittally, unwilling to voice an outright lie. Avoiding his gaze, she shifted uncomfortably in her seat.

"So why Peachville?" Mitch repeated his question. "I would have thought it would be a bit too quiet for you."

Abby frowned, unsure just what he meant. "I thought growing up in a small town like Peachville would be good for Toby. Lovely as Vancouver is, it's getting too big, too intimidating," she said, all the while thinking that her answer sounded lame.

"Peachville is a far cry from Vancouver, that's for sure," Mitch said. "But I agree with you. If I was a parent, I'd want my children to grow up right here, too."

At his words a wave of guilt washed over Abby, bringing with it the urge to blurt out the truth, but she bit down on the inner softness of her mouth and swallowed the confession suddenly hovering on her lips.

She turned to watch the passing scene, but the quiet beauty of the snow-covered fields seemed only to accentuate the silence that stretched between them like a rubber band waiting to snap.

"What about you? What brings *you* back?" Abby asked, unable to stand the tense silence a moment longer and wanting to shift the conversation to what she hoped would be a safer topic.

Mitch glanced at her briefly. "That's a very good question," he said. It was a question he'd asked himself a number of times throughout the early-morning drive from

Vancouver, only to reach the conclusion that the message Joyce had left on his answering machine had simply been the excuse he'd needed to come home.

After the nearly fatal conclusion to his last assignment, he needed time to think; time to take stock of his life; time to decide whether or not he wanted to continue in his chosen line of work.

Since completing his basic training he'd worked for the most part as an undercover officer. Initially he'd enjoyed the excitement that accompanied the job, and had felt a sense of pride and accomplishment whenever their work resulted in a hardened criminal being brought to justice.

But during the past year he'd grown weary of living under the constant fear of discovery, of always having to be on guard, and tired, too, of the fact that more and more often the criminals were walking out of court and back onto the streets laughing at the police all the way.

Mitch slowed the truck to a halt at the crossroads. He smiled ruefully at the irony. He was at a crossroads in his own life and feeling more than a little tentative about what lay ahead. As he made the turn toward Peachville he wished silently it was as easy to make life-changing choices.

"Actually, there are a number of reasons why I came back," Mitch said once he'd completed the turn. "One of them being that I thought it was as good a time as any to try and settle things between me and my father." His sigh was heartfelt. "Do you know he still refuses to believe that I visited my mother on the night she died? He insists that he never left her side." Pain and more than a hint of bitterness edged his voice now.

"But you were there," Abby blurted out, shocked at Mitch's revelation. "That was the night—" She broke off abruptly, and her hand flew to her mouth to stop the words *we made love* from escaping.

"That was the night you took pity on me," Mitch finished for her with a sharpness that had her head snapping around to look at him.

"Took pity on you?" Abby's heart felt as if it were being squeezed in a vise. Of all the emotions he'd aroused in her that night, pity hadn't been anywhere on the list.

"Suffice it to say, it was a mistake. It should never have happened," Mitch went on, his voice this time devoid of either inflection or emotion.

He turned to look at her and, as their eyes met, the air inside the cab crackled with renewed tension. "Isn't that what you told Cal?" he asked.

The question hung in the air like a guillotine waiting to fall, but Abby made no response because the pain twisting inside her made it impossible for her to speak.

Mitch switched his gaze to the road ahead and tightened his grip on the steering wheel, strangely moved by the wounded look he'd seen shimmering in the depths of her green eyes.

Who was she trying to fool? That night had meant nothing to her. How could it have when only a few months later she'd married another man? He'd been deceived once before by a look he'd seen in her eyes. Never again.

Silently he acknowledged that finding Abby in Peachville working for his father had unnerved him more than he was willing to admit. With her honey blond hair, flawless skin and haunting green eyes, she was still one of the most beautiful women he'd ever known.

But the compassion and comfort she'd so generously offered that night so long ago had been a lie, and he'd been forced to face the knowledge that he'd made a grave error in judgment, an error that still left a bitter taste in his mouth and a nagging ache in his heart.

Chapter Three

"Would it be all right if I dropped you off at the store and picked you up in...say, three quarters of an hour?" Mitch asked a short time later when he pulled in to the parking lot at the rear of Tennyson's Market.

"That's fine," Abby replied, relieved that he wouldn't be coming in with her. She was still trying to understand Mitch's comment that she'd taken pity on him that night, and still feeling astonished to learn of Tom's refusal to believe that Mitch had visited his mother on the night she died.

Should she talk to Tom and set the record straight? After all, she'd been on duty that night at the hospital. Her shift was scheduled to end at midnight, but it had been closer to one before she'd finally been able to leave. She'd come across Mitch wandering like a lost soul through the many corridors leading from one wing of the hospital to another.

She'd easily determined from the look of pain and despair on his face that he'd been to visit his mother, whose name Abby had noticed on the hospital's computer several days before.

When she'd approached him, he'd been murmuring incoherently, and she'd quickly realized from his agitated and almost tearful state that his mother's valiant and painful battle with cancer had ended.

"I'll let you out here," Mitch said as he brought the truck to a halt, effectively breaking into her reverie.

"Oh...right." Abby fumbled with the buckle of her seat belt before Mitch reached over and released it. "Thanks," she said, and, opening the door, climbed down from the truck.

"See you about eleven-thirty," Mitch said moments before she shut the door.

Abby put up her hand in acknowledgment of his words before carefully picking her way through the wet snow to the entrance of the store. Once inside she commandeered one of the small grocery buggies and, after fishing in her purse for the list she'd brought with her, headed toward the first aisle.

For the next thirty minutes Abby wound her way through the store surprised by the general state of disorder throughout. A number of shelves needed restocking, while others were untidy, with items scattered here and there. Though not a large or ultramodern store, Tennyson's was adequate in size, centrally located and in a relatively good state of repairs.

Abby had always liked and admired the way Tom had managed to preserve its unique character, which was not unlike an old-fashioned trading post. But as she continued to make her way up and down the narrow aisles, Abby was struck by the fact that there didn't appear to be many, if any, seasonal items either on sale or on display.

Abby remembered with affection the summer she'd been working in the store and how Tom had taken great pride in putting up rows of flags and rosettes to commemorate and celebrate the Fourth of July.

It seemed absurd, somehow, that there was no decorated Christmas tree, nor were there any decorations for sale—no candy canes, no tinsel, no snowmen or Santa Claus figures in sight, not even a colorful poinsettia. The general atmosphere throughout seemed to be one of bleakness rather than joyfulness in anticipation of the approaching Christmas holiday.

Tom's absence had undoubtedly played a factor in the store's neglected appearance, and Abby soon found herself wondering who was in charge. The store was in a disgraceful state, and she was sure if Tom knew, he would be both upset and angry at how quickly things had deteriorated during the three weeks he'd been away.

To the best of her recollection, the store had always been in good order whenever she'd come to shop. On her last visit, shortly after she and Toby had moved into Tom's house, she'd been in too much of a hurry and hadn't noticed anything amiss.

But as she pushed her laden buggy toward one of the six checkouts it was obvious from the hum of conversation going on around her that other customers had noticed the general disarray and were unhappy about the situation. Several people were in fact complaining rather loudly to one of the cashiers.

"I'm sorry, Mrs. Carstairs, but we're not taking orders for fresh turkeys this year," Abby heard the cashier say.

"It's a downright disgrace," came the customer's sharp reply. "Tom Tennyson has brought in fresh turkeys from the Simpson farm every year for as long as I can remember. I refuse to buy one of those frozen birds. How am I supposed to get my Christmas turkey if I can't order it here?"

"I don't know," the cashier replied. "I'm sorry," she added, looking upset.

"Who's in charge?" Mrs. Carstairs demanded. "I've a good mind to take my business elsewhere."

"Perhaps I can be of help, Mrs. Carstairs." The deep, resonant voice quickly captured everyone's attention and all eyes swung around to see Mitch, who had slipped into the store unnoticed in the commotion.

Abby felt her stomach muscles tighten and her heart skip a beat at the sight of him, and wondered vaguely if he had the same effect on every woman.

"Well, well! If it isn't Mitchell Tennyson," Mrs. Carstairs announced as a smile began to light up her features.

"In the flesh," Mitch replied, his eyes twinkling with humor.

"What the devil are you doing in Peachville?" she asked him.

"Right now I'm hoping to prevent one of my father's loyal and most valued customers from taking her business elsewhere," he responded lightly, though Abby heard the serious note in his voice. "Why don't you leave your buggy here for a minute, Mrs. Carstairs, and come with me to my father's office where you can tell me exactly what it is you're unhappy about?" He turned to the other customers still in line. "If any of you wish to make a complaint, please follow me."

Mitch's quiet tone and confident manner had a calming effect on everyone. Abby couldn't help but admire the way he'd taken control and defused what could easily have been an unpleasant situation.

As Mitch escorted Marilyn Carstairs and several other customers to the office, he noticed the general untidiness and air of disorder and felt his anger stir to life.

"I know your father's laid up in bed at the moment," Mrs. Carstairs said. "And I expect the reason no one has spoken up before now is because no one wants to worry him. But Tom would be appalled if he could see the state of the store. Just a month ago he was telling me all about the decorations he was planning to put up this year. But there don't appear to be any, and neither are there any other Christmas items." Out of breath, she came to a halt.

"Your father always took pride in bringing in quality novelty items at this time of year," commented another customer. "But I haven't found anything of that nature for sale in the store at all."

"I'll have to go somewhere else to get my table decorations and my Christmas crackers," a third lady announced.

"And can you believe it? Tennyson's not taking orders for fresh turkeys?" Mrs. Carstairs jumped into the fray again. "Why, it's ridiculous!"

"Your complaints are certainly valid," Mitch said as they reached the door of the office. "If you'll just bear with me, I'll do my best to find out what's been going on."

Mitch knocked on the door and opened it without waiting for a reply. Inside, a man in his late twenties sat in Tom's leather chair, his hands cupped behind his head, his feet on a desktop strewn with invoices and other papers.

Startled, the young man dropped his feet onto the floor and quickly stood, his face clearly expressing both surprise and annoyance at the intrusion.

"This is a private office. You can't come in here," he told Mitch.

"Are you in charge?" Mitch asked, barely managing to keep himself from grabbing the man by the front of his shirt.

"Yes, I am," came the curt reply.

"I have several customers here who have complaints that need attention," Mitch explained, curious to see just how the man would respond.

"Complaints?" the young man echoed, blinking several times.

"That's right," Mitch responded.

"Ah...well...you'll have to take any complaints directly to the store owner, Mr. Tennyson," the young man said, obviously flustered.

"Really," Mitch said lazily. "I assume you are aware that Mr. Tennyson broke his hip and is in the meantime at home recovering from the accident."

"Of course," came the reply.

"And you're actually suggesting that these customers should take their complaints to him?" Mitch's tone was icy now. "Tell me. What's your name?"

"Darren Erickson. Who are you?" came the terse and defensive reply.

"Mitch Tennyson. Tom Tennyson is my father," Mitch explained and at his words had the satisfaction of seeing Erickson's face pale slightly. "If you're in charge," Mitch calmly went on, "shouldn't *you* deal with these customers' complaints? And while you're at it, perhaps you could tell me why there are no Christmas items on the shelves and why the store is in such a state of disorder?''

"We're short staffed, that's why," Erickson blurted out. "Your father was supposed to hire extra help for the holidays, but he never got around to it."

"Why don't you hire them?" Mitch asked. "And as a stopgap measure, why aren't you out there sweeping the floor and stocking the shelves?" he challenged.

Erickson looked aghast at the suggestion. "That's not my job," he said. "I have more important things to take care of right here," he added, sweeping a hand in the direction of the paperwork heaped on the desktop.

"Really?" Mitch replied, his tone dripping with sarcasm.

"There's more to running a store than keeping the shelves stocked," Erickson retorted. "Look...I don't have time for this. I'm very busy. I must ask you all to leave."

"I don't think so," Mitch replied, slowly shaking his head. "If anyone's leaving, it's you. In fact, I insist."

"Insist? What do you mean?" Erickson demanded.

"You're fired!" Mitch said, and heard the murmur of approval that came from the small crowd behind him, who'd been listening with quiet fascination to the exchange.

"You can't fire me. Not without due cause," Erickson blundered, recovering quickly. "And anyway, you're not the owner," he said with a hint of smugness.

"I'm the owner's son, and in my father's absence I have full authority to fire whoever I please," Mitch enunciated carefully. "As for ample cause—the aisles need to be swept, shelves are in disarray and your refusal to address these customers' complaints all add up in my estimation to gross mismanagement." His tone was grim and uncompromising as he stared the younger man down. "You have exactly one minute to pick up your belongings and get out."

A look of anger and contempt flashed in Erickson's eyes and Mitch braced himself for an aggressive reaction. But as the seconds slowly ticked by, Erickson relaxed and a sneer began to curl at the corner of his mouth.

"You can keep your stupid job! Who needs it?" he said derisively as he reached around the door to grab his jacket.

Mitch turned to the small group of onlookers. "Excuse me while I escort Mr. Erickson to the door," he said.

"I know my way out," Erickson announced. Brushing past everyone, he headed down the nearest aisle.

Mitch ignored his comment and, keeping pace with Erickson, walked with him to the front of the store.

Abby had just finished paying the cashier when she saw Mitch and Darren Erickson approach. From their grim expressions, she had the strong impression something dramatic had occurred. She continued to watch as both men strode purposefully past the row of cashiers toward the exit.

Darren Erickson came to a halt when he reached the automatic doors. As they opened for him, he turned to face Mitch. "I'll sue for wrongful dismissal," Erickson said in an obvious last-ditch effort to save face.

"Go right ahead," Mitch challenged. "You don't have a leg to stand on."

"Tell that to my lawyer," Erickson said with a smirk. "Anyway, this place is a dump. Your old man should have sold it when he had the chance," he added nastily.

"I'll mail whatever is owed to you. Don't bother coming back," Mitch said evenly, his dislike of Erickson growing by leaps and bounds.

"It's a free country. I can do what I like," Erickson sneered. Spinning on his heel, he walked out without a backward glance.

Mitch had to stifle the urge to go after Erickson. But even if he'd had the authority, he could hardly arrest a man for laziness or incompetence. No crime, at least none that he was aware of, had been committed.

"What was that all about?" Abby asked as she came up behind him.

"I fired him," Mitch explained, slowly feeling the tension inside him begin to ease.

"Fired him?" she repeated.

"That's right," Mitch responded. "Why anyone would hire a jerk like that in the first place is beyond me." He was silent for a moment, his expression thoughtful. "Have you heard my father say anything about selling the store?" he asked.

Abby frowned. "No...he's never mentioned it," she said. "At least, not to me. It's not true, is it?"

"I hope not," Mitch replied, bothered more than he was willing to admit by the idea that his father might be considering selling Tennyson's Market. The store had been in the family for several generations and was regarded as a historic landmark in Peachville.

"I've finished shopping," Abby said. "Are you ready to go?"

"Actually, no," Mitch said. "Now that I've fired Erickson there's a few things I need to take care of around here before I can leave, including those customers waiting for me in the office." His eyes darted in that direction before meeting hers once more. "Look, Abby, why don't you drive my truck home? I'll see if I can get a ride from someone later."

"Are you sure?" Abby asked, reluctant to leave.

Mitch dug into the pocket of his jeans and extracted his keys. "It's parked right out front," he said, handing them to her. "Tell my father I'm staying to help out at the store for a while. I'll see you back at the house." Without waiting for a reply, he turned and walked away.

Abby curled her fingers around the keys and watched as Mitch strode past the cashiers toward the rear of the store. Outside, she was met with a cold blast from the icy winter wind, which was blowing the snow already on the ground into small drifts in the parking lot. Though it wasn't snowing hard, Abby had a feeling it was only a matter of time.

After loading the groceries into the back seat of the truck, Abby climbed into the cab, but instead of starting the engine she sat for several minutes watching as a stream of customers entered the store.

Undoubtedly the predicted change in the weather had prompted a few townsfolk to make a trip to the store in preparation for the approaching storm. Tom would be fine for a few hours, she told herself. And the more Abby thought about the state of Tennyson's Market, the more she didn't feel right about leaving Mitch to tackle the situation on his own.

When she'd worked at Tennyson's that summer so long ago, she'd often helped out by stocking shelves and sweeping the floor, and she was reasonably sure she knew where the storage cupboard was and where all the cleaning items were kept. Her decision made, she climbed down from the cab and locked the door.

There was no sign of Mitch as she reentered the building, and the cashiers were too busy to even notice her return. Feeling sure Mitch would decline her offer to help, she avoided the office as she made her way to the rear of the store. Pushing open the doors leading to the storage area, she glanced around, relieved to note that nothing much had changed.

Sliding off her coat, she hung it up, replacing it with a large apron with Tennyson's Market printed across the bib. From the cleaning cupboard she took one of the wide sweeping mops used to clean the floor, and pushing a large garbage bin on wheels ahead of her through the swing doors, she began to clean and dust the aisles, one at a time.

After Abby finished this task, she began replenishing stock on some of the empty shelves. She was asked several times by customers for a specific item and managed after a search to locate the item required.

Each time she'd passed the door to Tom Tennyson's office she'd caught a glimpse of Mitch talking on the telephone or flipping through the papers on his father's desk, but he hadn't looked up.

Unwilling to disturb or interrupt him, she'd reasoned that if Mitch did happen to leave the store he was bound to notice his truck, put two and two together and realize that she was waiting for him.

Returning to the storeroom once more, Abby noticed several boxes on one of the top shelves, with the words Christmas Decorations written in black ink on the side. After locating a small stepladder she decided to bring down the boxes and check their contents.

* * *

As Mitch made his way to the front of the store he noticed that the floor of the aisle had been swept and several shelves had been tidied and restocked. Puzzled, he glanced at the cashiers, noting that all five girls were busy ringing through customers. Turning down another aisle, Mitch headed for the storeroom, curious to find out which of his father's twelve employees had been blessed with a strong sense of responsibility as well as initiative.

Pushing open the door of the storeroom, he came to an abrupt halt at the sight of Abby teetering rather precariously on the third rung of a stepladder.

His breath constricted in his throat as his eyes made the journey up the long jean-clad legs to the firm, nicely rounded buttocks, past the slender waist to the honey blond hair falling like a sun-drenched waterfall onto her shoulders.

Free from the confines of the knot at the nape of her neck, her hair looked like spun gold, and his fingers suddenly itched to touch, to stroke, to feel again the silky softness that had stirred his senses and stolen his reason that night so long ago.

"Abby! What the hell are you doing here?" Mitch demanded, annoyed at himself and the route his thoughts had taken.

At the sound of Mitch's gruff tone, Abby glanced over her shoulder, an action that caused her foot to slip off the narrow rung of the ladder.

"Oh..." Abby moaned as she started to fall backward.

With quicksilver reflexes Mitch closed the gap between them. Planting his hands on either side of her waist, he managed to steady her. "You'd better come down off that thing," he instructed, his voice sounding strained. "Just take it one step at a time."

With her heart beating a wild tattoo against her breast Abby made her descent, conscious all the while of Mitch's hands circling her waist. Once on the ground she felt her knees buckle for a split second—delayed shock, she told herself—and she bumped awkwardly against Mitch's broad chest. At the contact Abby heard his muffled grunt and saw his face contort briefly in pain.

Puzzled, her eyes flew to meet his, but as their glances collided, the air between them was suddenly rife with tension.

"I thought I told you to go home," Mitch said irritably, fighting the urge to cover her mouth with his, wondering what there was about this woman that set his blood humming through his veins.

"You did," Abby replied, her tone breathless, her skin tingling beneath the heat of his hands.

"Then why are you still here?" Mitch abruptly released her and ran a hand through his hair, angry at himself and his response.

Abby took a step back. "I decided to stick around and give you a hand. You probably don't remember, but back when I was in high school I worked in your father's store one summer," she told him.

"I remember," Mitch said. "So you're the one responsible for sweeping the floor," he went on, surprise evident in his voice.

"And I restocked some of the shelves," she informed him archly, irked by his tone and strangely hurt that the idea of her helping should seem so preposterous to him.

"My father hired you to look after him," Mitch said, anger and another emotion less easy to define simmering just below the surface.

Abby felt her eyes sting with tears and she quickly blinked them away. "You're absolutely right," she said, managing to keep her voice even. "You obviously don't want or need my help. If you'll excuse me, I'd better get back to your father." Turning from him, she crossed to retrieve her coat.

Mitch cursed under his breath. "Abby, wait!" he said, but she ignored him. Shoulders rigid, back stiff, she pulled on her coat. Though he knew he'd been deliberately and unreasonably unkind, that he should be thanking her for the work she'd done, he was still trying to deal with his body's reaction to her, annoyed to discover that even after all this time she still had the power to affect him. "Abby, I'm sorry," he said. "I was out of line."

Abby came to a halt at the swing doors, but she didn't turn to look at him.

Mitch inhaled deeply before continuing. "I've just spent the past hour and more trying to find out what's been going on around here," he told her. "I had no right to take my frustrations out on you. I'm sorry. I really appreciate what you've done."

This time Abby turned to face him. "Apology accepted," she said. "But you're right. Your father did hire me to look after him. I'd better get back."

"Are you hungry?" Mitch asked suddenly.

Abby frowned. "A little. Why?" she replied, puzzled by his sudden change of subject.

Mitch glanced at his watch. "It's only one o'clock," he said. "You left a lunch for my father. He should be all right for another hour, don't you think? The least I can do is take you to lunch."

"Really, it's not necessary," Abby insisted, wishing now she'd ignored the impulse that had sent her back into the store.

"It is for me," Mitch returned. "I'm famished." If the truth be known Mitch felt nauseous and a little dizzy. When he'd discharged himself from the hospital in Toronto two days ago the doctors had warned him not to overtire or overexert himself. The feeling of weakness assailing him now was quite probably due to the collision with Abby and the fact that he wasn't adhering to the doctor's strict orders to rest in bed and eat regularly. The oatmeal he'd eaten earlier had long since worn off.

Abby had the good grace not to argue, and five minutes later found them sitting across from each other in a tiny bistro a short walk from Tennyson's Market.

"This place must be new," Mitch commented as he slid off his parka and hung it over the back of his chair.

"Yes, it is," Abby confirmed, doing the same with her coat. "It opened a few months ago after undergoing some minor renovations. Rumor has it the chef once worked in a hotel in San Francisco."

Mitch finished browsing through the menu and glanced around with interest, liking the cosy atmosphere, especially the flickering flames of the gas fire in the brick fireplace against the wall.

The waitress arrived to take their order and Abby opted for a large bowl of homemade tomato basil soup and a freshly baked cheese bun. Mitch also chose the soup along with a clubhouse sandwich.

Once the waitress left, Abby gazed across the table at Mitch, noting the lines of strain on his handsome features. "Did you find out if your father is planning to sell the store?" she asked, capturing his attention.

"No," Mitch replied. "I spent most of the time going through the employee records and trying to make sense of the schedule. What a mess! Erickson didn't have a clue how to make up a work schedule. I still don't understand why my father hired him." He paused for a moment then continued. "I called a couple of the guys who normally work in the stockroom. After I told them who I was and that I'd fired Erickson, they both agreed to come in later."

"That's good," Abby commented.

"Hopefully everything will soon be back on track," Mitch said with a sigh. "But I'm still at a loss to know what's happened to all the Christmas items."

"I saw some boxes in the stockroom marked Christmas Decorations," Abby remarked. "That's why I was climbing the ladder," she explained.

"I see. Well, that's something," he said, his tone a little more cheerful. "My father always prided himself in creating just the right atmosphere in the store, getting into the spirit of whichever holiday or season it happened to be. I don't think I've ever seen the place looking so bare and unwelcoming."

"I know what you mean," Abby agreed.

"Dad deserves a lot of credit for the market's success. Being the only store in town for a long time helped, of course," Mitch acknowledged. "But he's always considered it his pride and joy." He shook his head. "My mother used to complain that he spent more time at the market than at home." Mitch's mouth curved in a smile at the memory. "Mother was teasing, of course, but Dad was never quite sure, and on the nights he was late for dinner, he'd bring home a bouquet of fresh flowers for her. I think she said it to get the flowers."

Abby felt her throat tighten with emotion when she heard the love in his voice for the woman who had given him life. "You still miss her," Abby said softly, and glimpsed the glint of moisture in his eyes as he met her gaze.

"Yes, I still miss her," he admitted, his voice thick with emotion as he gazed into eyes as green and fathomless as the ocean. The dizziness he'd experienced earlier swamped him once more and he had to close his eyes to combat the feeling.

"Mitch? Are you all right?" Abby asked, noticing now with a twinge of alarm that his face had gone quite pale and the lines of strain around his mouth seemed more pronounced.

"I'm fine," he replied, and even managed a smile, but in truth he was far from fine and he knew it.

The waitress chose that moment to appear with two steaming bowls of soup and it was not without some relief that Mitch reached for the spoon. After several mouthfuls of the creamy aromatic soup he began to feel marginally better. "I called the Simpson farm about the turkeys," Mitch said a few moments later.

"The turkeys?" Abby repeated, regarding him with a frown.

"Dad always orders fresh turkeys from the Simpson farm every Christmas, but only for those customers who ask. Mrs. Carstairs is one of those customers and she was complaining earlier that no one at the store would take her order."

"I see," Abby said.

"Steve Simpson said he'd called to ask if there were any orders, but Erickson told him he wouldn't be needing any fresh turkeys, that he'd ordered more frozen ones. Steve said he was a bit surprised but other than calling my father, there wasn't much he could do."

Mitch scooped another spoonful of the soup into his mouth. "From what I could garner from the papers in the office, Erickson was just downright lazy," he went on, carefully returning the spoon to the soup bowl. "With my father in the hospital there wasn't anyone around to either direct him or supervise. Suddenly finding himself thrust into the position of running the entire store on his own must have been daunting for Erickson. I can almost feel sorry for him," he said. "It's my guess he couldn't handle all the pressures and simply took the easy way out by deciding to keep a low profile and do as little as possible, which included ignoring the fact that it was Christmas."

"Just like Scrooge," Abby said, and at her comment saw a ghost of a smile flicker across Mitch's face.

"Luckily, there's time enough to set most things right," Mitch commented. "Christmas is one of the busiest times of the year for any store. I'm sure Dad's regular customers will remain loyal, but I just hope, for his sake, he hasn't already lost too much business elsewhere." He pushed his plate away, annoyance simmering through him once more at the damage Erickson had done. "I really need to talk to my father, tell him what's happened. If I know him, he'll have a thing or two to say about Erickson."

"This could be the incentive he needs to get out of bed," Abby said.

"You might be right," Mitch replied. "In any case there isn't too much more I can do until I talk to him." He rose from the chair.

"You didn't finish your soup," Abby observed. "I thought you were hungry. Aren't you going to eat the sandwich you ordered? The waitress is bringing it now."

"Could you wrap that up for me?" Mitch asked when the waitress reached them.

"Of course, sir," came the reply before she turned and hurriedly retraced her steps.

As Mitch yanked his parka from the back of the chair with his left hand, a pain—sharp and intense—had him gasping. Steadying himself against the back of the chair, he was almost sure, judging by the painful throbbing in his chest and the warm wetness accompanying it, that his wound had just started to bleed again.

Cursing under his breath at his own foolishness, he gritted his teeth and carefully eased his arm into the sleeve of his parka, trying not to think of the Toronto doctor's angry tirade over Mitch's decision to check himself out.

Abby grabbed her coat and followed Mitch to the cashier. She'd noticed the tightening of his mouth as he stood, and noted, too, the slow deliberate way he'd donned his jacket. He was in pain, she was sure of it, and his pale features and clenched jaw only served to confirm her suspicion.

Throughout the short journey back to the truck, Abby had the distinct impression Mitch's pace had slowed and she noted that his breathing appeared labored.

Climbing into the passenger seat, she tugged at the seat belt and popped it into place.

"Abby?" Mitch's voice coming from the driver's side was low and faintly husky.

Puzzled by his tone, she turned to him. "Yes?"

"I think you'd better drive," he said a split second before he slumped forward, unconscious, onto the steering wheel.

Chapter Four

"Mitch? Mitch!" Abby fumbled with her seat belt, finally freeing herself from its confines. Sliding closer to Mitch's limp body, she clutched at his jacket and with an effort managed to pull him off the steering wheel.

As he slumped back against the upholstery she gently patted his cheek, all the while willing herself to stay calm. She was a nurse, trained to deal with situations of this kind, but somehow the fact that Mitch was the man unconscious beside her added a complication she could well have done without.

Unzipping his parka, she slid her hand inside, placing it over his heart, and immediately felt the life-affirming beat against her palm. Relief flooded through her and she quickly turned her attention to his breathing, which appeared slow but quite normal.

He'd fainted. That was her diagnosis. But she was at a loss to understand the reason. Though she'd been almost sure he'd been hurt in some fashion, she could see no evidence to support that theory. And that was the part that worried her.

"Mitch, wake up!" she urged as she patted his cheek, a little harder this time. She watched as his eyelids fluttered briefly, indicating that he was not in a deep state of unconsciousness.

"Mitch." Abby spoke his name again and this time his eyes opened and stayed open. He gazed at her bemusedly for several seconds.

"What happened?" The question sounded slurred, as though he'd been drinking too much.

"For some unaccountable reason, you fainted," she told him with an exasperated sigh. "I think I'd better take you to the hospital," she added.

"No! I'll be all right." His speech was clearer now, his eyes focused. He clutched at her arm as he met her gaze.

"Mitch, if you're hurt, as I suspect you are, you should see a doctor," Abby said, concern for him evident in her voice.

"I already did. He told me I'd be fine," Mitch insisted. "I just feel a bit woozy, that's all. I'm all right," he repeated as if to convince himself. "You can drive my truck, can't you?"

"You've seen a doctor?" Abby ignored his question, intent on finding out what was wrong with him.

He nodded. "A few days ago, in Toronto," he told her. "I had a run-in with a creep brandishing a knife," he stated calmly. "Unfortunately, I wasn't quick enough on my feet and I ended up needing a couple of stitches."

"Are you telling me you were stabbed?" Abby asked as a chill danced down her spine in reaction.

"It's only a scratch. I'll live," Mitch answered, fighting to control the nausea threatening to drag him under once more. Silently he admonished himself for not heeding the doctor's warnings about overdoing it. But once he'd left the hospital he'd had other things on his mind. "I just need to lie down for a while," he said. "Take me home.... Please, Abby."

Abby stared at him for a long moment. His face looked gray with pain and fatigue and Abby sensed he was downplaying the seriousness of his injury. Her instincts were telling her she should drive him to the hospital, but she couldn't ignore the plea she could see in the depths of his pale blue eyes.

"This is against my better judgment," she began with a shake of her head, and watched as Mitch's eyes closed in obvious relief. "If you want me to drive, we're going to have to trade places. I'll go around. Can you slide across to the passenger side?" she asked as she reached for the door handle.

"No problem," she heard Mitch say before she opened the door and jumped down into the wet snow. As she walked around the truck, an image of Mitch fighting off a knife-wielding thug filled her mind and a shudder that had nothing to do with the falling temperatures vibrated through her, bringing her momentarily to a halt.

From the matter-of-fact way he'd spoken she'd had the impression that facing knife-wielding criminals was commonplace, but even though she'd been married to a police officer and knew they risked their lives to uphold the law, she doubted she'd ever become as blasé as Mitch appeared to be about the dangers they faced each and every day.

Cal, for one, had found that aspect of the job exciting. He'd thrived on what he'd described as "living on the edge." But Abby had soon realized the man she'd married harbored a cruel streak, taking pleasure in the power his uniform afforded him, enjoying being able to intimidate others.

He'd used that power on her, although his intimidation tactics had been much more subtle. She'd walked blindly into his trap, and she had only herself to blame for believing him when he told her he cared, for believing him when he vowed that he only had her unborn child's welfare at heart, for believing him when he'd told her marriage to him was the best solution.

Abby thrust those dark memories aside and, pulling her coat more tightly around her, she reached the driver's door. She climbed into the cab and Mitch, still conscious, flashed her the ghost of a smile as she snapped on her seat belt and started the engine.

After carefully negotiating her way out of the parking spot, she made the turn toward home. Glancing periodically at her passenger, Abby was relieved to see Mitch's color gradually improve, due no doubt to the warm air blasting from the truck's heater. Though he drifted in and out of consciousness throughout the journey, she felt reasonably sure he was in no danger.

Outside, the wind was beginning to pick up, playfully tossing snow at the truck in swirling handfuls. Here and there on the road Abby saw the glitter of ice and was glad Mitch had had the foresight to have chains put on his tires, giving better traction on the slippery roads.

Dark, threatening storm clouds continued to build in the sky, but other than a few flurries of snow, they made the return trip without a hitch.

"We're home," Abby said as she brought the truck to a halt near the front door. Beside her Mitch gave no indication that he'd heard. Abby jumped out and came around to open the passenger door. As the cold blast of winter air invaded the truck's interior, Mitch stirred and murmured sleepily.

"Mitch, wake up." Abby gently nudged him and his eyes slowly opened.

"Hi," he said softly, his lips curving into a warm smile.

"Hi, yourself," Abby replied, ignoring the leap her pulse took in response to his lazy smile. "Mitch, you're going to have to help me," she told him.

"Home already?" he asked, his glance sliding past her to the front door. "That was fast."

"Come on," she said, and waited until he'd eased himself from the cab to stand beside her in the snow. "Lean on me," she instructed.

"I can manage," he assured her, but as he took a step, dizziness assailed him. "Damn it!" he muttered under his breath.

"Don't be so stubborn. Lean on me," Abby ordered, putting her arm around him.

Abby unlocked the front door and instantly the warmth from the house enveloped them like a big bear hug. By the time they'd negotiated the stairs and reached Mitch's bedroom, perspiration was beading his forehead.

"Let me help you take off your parka," Abby said.

"No...thanks," Mitch quickly cut in. "You've done more than enough. I'll be fine," he said, gingerly lowering himself onto the edge of his bed as the dull ache throbbed insistently in his side.

"You're not fine," Abby insisted, refusing to be put off. "I'm a nurse, remember? I agreed not to take you to the hospital, but I think you should let me take a look at your wound. It might need attention."

"It's really not necessary," Mitch said.

"I'll be the judge of that," Abby countered, refusing to be put off.

Mitch met her gaze and knew he was fighting a losing battle. "Fine...." He grudgingly relented. "Just give me a few minutes, all right?"

Abby held his gaze for a long moment, then nodded. "I'll check on your father, bring in the groceries, then I'll be back," she said before making her way from the room.

Peeking in on Tom, she saw that he'd eaten the sandwich she'd left and was enjoying a nap. She quietly withdrew and headed downstairs, where she quickly unloaded the groceries from the back seat of the truck.

Removing her coat, she put away the perishable items in the fridge, leaving the remaining items to deal with later. After heating some water in the microwave she dropped a tea bag into the cup and added a liberal amount of sugar. Cup in hand, she collected her first aid kit and hurried upstairs.

Mitch, minus his parka and shirt but still wearing his jeans, lay on top of the quilt, his eyes closed. A shiver of awareness danced down Abby's spine and she felt her stomach muscles tighten at the sight of his bare chest with its sprinkling of dark hairs forming a pattern that disappeared beneath the waistband of his jeans.

Annoyed at her reaction, Abby firmly put a cap on her emotions, telling herself repeatedly that he was just another patient. Setting the hot tea and her first aid kit on the table by the bedside, she glanced at his naked chest once more, this time noting with cool control the dressing taped to his left side, just below his armpit.

The bandage was stained with blood, but the stain hadn't spread far, an indication that the stitches he'd told her about hadn't ruptured. But to minimize the chance of infection, the dressing needed changing.

Trying not to wake Mitch, Abby reached across his body and as gently as she could started to ease off the strips of adhesive tape holding the soiled dressing in place.

At the touch of her fingers against his skin Mitch's eye flew open and he sucked in a breath in startled reaction.

Abby instantly withdrew. "Sorry," she said, thinking she must have hurt him. "How do you feel?" she asked, scanning his handsome features once more. "I've brought you some tea."

Mitch slowly released the breath trapped in his lungs. "Ah...weak and sleepy just about covers it," he responded, glad he was lying down.

"Try and drink some tea before you drift off to sleep again," Abby suggested. "While you do that I'll change your dressing and make sure your stitches are still intact."

"I'll have the tea in a minute," Mitch murmured. Closing his eyes, he braced himself for the ordeal to come.

All at once the sweet scent of lilacs assailed his senses as Abby leaned over him. Several strands of her hair brushed his chest to torment and tease, making him wonder if he wasn't being subjected to some ancient, erotic torture.

Her touch was feather light and infinitely seductive, awakening long-forgotten needs and sending delicious tremors racing across his flesh.

Curling his hands into the quilt, he held his body taut as she slowly began to peel back the dressing. Though he kept his eyes shut tight, he knew the exact moment she leaned in for a closer look at the wound.

His stomach muscles quivered from the effort to keep still, and when her warm breath fanned the hairs on his chest, the resulting ripples of sensation sent his blood pressure soaring.

"There's been some minor seepage from the wound, but the stitches themselves are still intact," she told him.

"Good." The word wheezed from between his clenched jaw as he struggled to control his body's overwhelming response to the woman before him. His system felt as if it had been rocked by a small earthquake and even in his weak-

ened state it was all he could do not to capture her quest-
ing hands and press them to his lips.

"This might hurt."

Mitch barely heard her warning, but he welcomed the
brief spasm of pain as she tugged off the remainder of the
dressing, which effectively diverted his attention from the
desire urgently making itself known.

"The worst is over," Abby assured him, but silently
Mitch wondered how much more he could take.

Permitting Abby to minister to him had been a mistake.
With each breath he was assaulted with the scent that had
stirred his senses so long ago, the scent that could excite him
as no other could, the scent that was hers alone.

The memory of how she'd responded in his arms that
night, of the fiery passion they'd shared, still haunted his
dreams. But when the whisperings had reached him that he
hadn't been the only man to enjoy the intimate secrets of
her body, he'd been stunned and deeply crushed.

And although he'd tried to bury the memory of that
night in the deepest recesses of his heart, he'd never been
able to forget her, or fully understand the feeling she'd
aroused in him.

Abby glanced at the wound and was relieved to note that
there were no signs of infection. Though the cut looked a
little red and rather ugly, someone had done a good job of
sewing.

Gazing at the bruised flesh around the wound, Abby
couldn't prevent the tremor that rocked her at the realization that, had the knife been but a few inches lower and
nearer the center of his chest, the outcome could well have
been vastly different. Mitch could have died.

But he hadn't died. He was alive. Very much alive, she
thought as she let her gaze travel freely over the muscular
planes of his naked chest. Throughout the procedure she'd
managed to maintain a professional attitude, but all at once
her fingers itched to explore the sculpted contours of his
chest, to reacquaint themselves with the strength and
smoothness of his muscular shoulders, as well as the
springy softness of his chest hair.

"All done?" Mitch asked, and at his question Abby almost jumped out of her skin. Heat blazed across her face and she glanced at Mitch, prepared to see a look of derision in the pale depths of his eyes. To her relief his eyes were still closed.

"Yes," she managed to say as she bent to gather up the first aid kit. "Drink the tea and then get some rest," she told him, but her words garnered no reply other than the sound of his deep, steady breathing.

Abby gazed down at Mitch's sleeping figure for a long moment before pulling the quilt over him. Closing the bedroom door behind her, she crossed the hall and peeked into Tom's room to confirm he was still dozing.

After returning the first aid kit to the bathroom cupboard, Abby headed for the kitchen to put away the remainder of the dry goods. That done, she glanced at the clock on the wall, noting she had an hour before the school bus dropped Toby off, time enough to prepare the evening meal and make a batch of Toby's favorite cookies.

It was later, as she began to gather the ingredients needed to make the chocolate chip cookies for Toby, that she found her thoughts drifting to those moments in Mitch's bedroom. As she measured the flour and sugar into a bowl, she recalled with a pang the sudden and almost overwhelming urge to feel again the warmth and silky texture of Mitch's skin beneath her fingers.

That she was still strongly attracted to him came as no surprise. Resolutely she reminded herself that he'd hurt her deeply seven years ago when he'd made love to her then left like a thief in the night without as much as a goodbye. But silently she had to admit that she'd never been able to forget the depths of passion or the heights of ecstasy she'd known in his arms.

Their passionate encounter, however, had meant nothing more to Mitch than a one-night stand. That he believed she'd simply taken pity on him that night added insult to the emotional injuries he'd already inflicted, and she vowed never to let Mitch, or anyone for that matter, get close enough to break her heart a second time.

The sound of the front door opening cut into Abby's musing and, dropping the last of the cookie mix onto a cookie sheet, she popped two trays into the oven.

"Mom! I'm home," Toby called as he came rushing into the kitchen.

Abby's heart melted at the sight of her rosy-cheeked son, his eyes sparkling with excitement.

"Cookies! Neat-o!" Toby's blue eyes, a shade darker than his father's, widened at the sight of Abby's first batch of freshly baked cookies cooling on a plate.

"Hi, sweetheart," Abby greeted her son. "Yes, they're cookies," she confirmed with a teasing grin. "Did you have a good day at school?" she asked as she crossed to the fridge and removed a carton of milk.

Toby climbed up onto a kitchen chair and helped himself to a cookie. "Yeah. We had a rehearsal of the Christmas play after lunch," he said, taking a big bite. "It was fun." His words were slightly muffled. "My friend Norman, he's playing the part of Joseph, tripped on his costume and nearly fell off the stage," Toby told her, laughter ringing in his voice.

"I hope he didn't hurt himself," Abby said.

Toby shook his head, still munching. "Mrs. Spracklin brought a gold-colored costume in for me. It looks cool," he added seconds before stuffing the remnants of the cookie into his mouth.

"That was nice of her," Abby responded as she retrieved a glass from the cupboard.

Toby swallowed the last morsel. "We sang some carols, too," he hurried on, already reaching for a second cookie. "After the play is over, the audience is supposed to join in and sing some carols with us."

"Sounds like fun,' Abby said, smiling as she filled the glass.

"Where's Mitch?" Toby asked, and at his question Abby felt a pain clutch at her heart. She was silent for a moment as she watched the milk swirling in the glass.

"He's resting," she said.

"Resting?" Toby repeated in a puzzled tone, taking another bite of cookie.

"Yes," Abby said without elaborating. "Is it snowing yet?" she asked, changing the subject, unwilling to get into a discussion about Mitch. But Toby had other ideas.

"Not yet," Toby replied. "Did Mitch tell you I beat him to the bus stop this morning?" he asked.

"No," Abby answered.

"Mrs. Mac looked so surprised when she saw him. She even got out of the bus and gave him a hug. All the kids were laughing," Toby went on, smiling at the memory.

"Here's your milk," Abby said, setting the glass on the counter.

"Thanks," said Toby. "Mitch told us that Mrs. Mac sat in front of him when he went to school and he used to pull her hair," he continued.

"Really," Abby responded dryly, surprised that she should feel hurt that Toby obviously found the man who was his father fun and amusing.

"Can I go see if he's finished resting?" Toby asked before taking several big gulps of milk.

"No!" Abby responded, and saw Toby's eyes widen at the sharpness in her voice. "He's sleeping," she added softly. "I think we should just let him rest."

"Okay." Toby accepted her suggestion. "How many cookies can I have?" he asked, his hand already hovering over the plate as he waited for her answer.

"Three's the limit," Abby replied. "I'm going to take Tom his tea and a couple of those cookies before you eat them all." She moved to pick up the tray.

"Can I have four?" Toby asked, a pleading look in his eyes.

"All right, but only if you set the table for me," she said over her shoulder.

Upstairs Abby nudged open the door to Tom's bedroom with the edge of the tray. "Good...you're awake," she said as she entered. "I thought you might be ready for a cup of tea and some freshly baked chocolate chip cookies."

"I thought I could smell cookies baking," Tom commented, easing himself into a sitting position. "Thanks, Abby," he added as she set the tray on his lap. "Where's Mitch?"

"In his room," Abby replied, wondering why Mitch's whereabouts should be of such interest to both Toby and Tom.

"Was everything all right at the market?" Tom asked. "How do the Christmas decorations in the store look?"

Abby was silent as she bent to retrieve the pillow that had fallen to the floor. Plumping it up, she set it behind Tom's head.

Tom glanced at her, his face creasing into a frown. "Is something wrong at the store?" he asked, a hint of anxiety creeping into his voice.

"Nothing that can't be set right." The comment came from Mitch, who'd appeared in the open doorway.

Abby's pulse began to skip a little faster as she turned to look at him. She was pleased to note that the lines of strain around his mouth had almost disappeared.

"What do you mean, nothing that can't be set right?" Tom demanded, his gaze jumping from Mitch to Abby and back to Mitch again. "What needs setting right? Erickson knows what to do. I went over everything a dozen times with him."

"A dozen wasn't quite enough," Mitch said, keeping his tone light, seeing that his father's face was beginning to turn red.

"You're talking in riddles, boy," Tom said. "Say what you mean and mean what you say. Now, tell me. What the devil has Erickson been up to?"

"Nothing," Mitch replied. "That's just it. He hasn't done a thing. That's why I fired him."

Tom stared at his son in astonishment. "You fired him?"

"Yes," Mitch said. "And I'd be interested to know why you hired him in the first place."

"And when did I put you in charge?" his father wanted to know.

Abby, fearful the exchange might become heated, quickly jumped into the fray. "Tom, please don't upset yourself. Mitch only did what you would have done. There are no Christmas decorations anywhere in the store, not on display or for sale," she told him. "And several customers were complaining to the cashier."

Tom stared at Abby. "No decorations? But that's impossible. I always have decorations.... I don't understand."

"I'm sorry, Dad," Mitch said, moving to stand at the foot of the bed. "I went to your office, along with a few customers, to talk to Erickson. His attitude left a lot to be desired and he as much as told me to mind my own business. I hadn't much option but to fire him."

Tom relaxed against the pillows, his anger spent. "I knew Erickson was lazy, because I had to hound him all the time to get him to do anything, but I never thought—" He broke off and glanced at his son. "I hired him because he was the only one who applied for the job."

"I see," Mitch said soberly. "Well, maybe if we put our heads together on this, we can straighten things out."

Picking up a cookie from the plate, Tom bit into it, his expression thoughtful.

Abby glanced at the plate. "Oh...that reminds me, I still have a batch of cookies in the oven. I'll leave you two to sort things out," she said as she crossed to the door. "Dinner will be ready in an hour."

As she made her way to the kitchen Abby felt encouraged by the fact that while tempers had flared briefly between Mitch and his father, their mutual interest in the welfare of the store gave them common ground on which to work. It was a start.

Toby was nowhere in sight when Abby returned to the kitchen. After removing the last tray of cookies from the oven she set them on a rack to cool, then popped into the oven the chicken casserole she'd prepared earlier.

As she cleaned up and cleared away the cooking utensils, she was pleased to note that Toby had set the table with three place settings, a napkin at each setting. Abby could hear the faint hum of voices coming from the television set in the living room and knew that Toby was watching one of his favorite after-school shows.

A flicker of moment by the window caught her attention and she glanced outside to see giant white snowflakes dancing past and settling on the ground below. The storm the forecasts had promised was finally putting in an appearance and, judging by the size of the flakes and the speed they were falling, Abby had a feeling it wouldn't be long before the landscape vanished beneath a thick white winter blanket.

It was still snowing an hour later as Abby checked the vegetables simmering on the stove. In the interim she'd taken a quick shower and traded her jeans for a pair of navy wool slacks and a dusty pink sweater. After blow-drying her hair, she'd twisted it into a loose knot at the nape of her neck.

"Something smells good."

At the sound of Mitch's voice a shiver of sensation skimmed across her nerve endings. Keeping her expression neutral, Abby turned to him. "Take a seat. Dinner will only be another five minutes," she told him. "I'm getting your father's tray ready."

"Where's Toby?" Mitch asked as he crossed to the counter.

"Washing his hands," Abby replied.

Mitch let his glance sweep over Abby, taking in the pink sweater that accentuated the rounded curve of her breasts. That she'd showered and changed was apparent, and suddenly he wished he'd done the same, though he wasn't quite sure how he'd have managed to prevent the clean dressing Abby had applied from getting soaked.

The hour he'd spent with his father had proved to be informative and productive. For the first time in too long they'd managed to have a discussion without their emotions and personal feelings getting in the way.

The fact that the discussion had centered on the market and the problems Erickson had created had undoubtedly been the reason for the brief cease-fire they'd enjoyed. And while Mitch had been tempted to turn the conversation to the subject of his mother's death, he'd resisted the impulse, reminding himself that Rome wasn't built in a day, and there would be time enough during the next few weeks to set his father straight on a number of things.

"Hi, Mitch." The greeting came from Toby, who joined them in the kitchen.

Mitch flashed the youngster a smile. ''Hi, Toby. How's it going?''

''Fine,'' Toby replied.

''Toby, put this bowl of vegetables on the table for me, please,'' Abby interrupted, handing the dish to her son. ''I'll take Mr. Tom's tray up and be right back,'' she said, already making her way out of the kitchen.

When Abby returned a few minutes later it was in time to hear the sound of shared laughter. Her heart leapt into her throat at the sight of Toby and Mitch, grinning at each other across the table like two mischievous boys. The resemblance between father and son was uncanny and it was all Abby could do to prevent the fear suddenly gripping her from showing on her face.

''Is something wrong?'' Mitch asked, puzzled by the expression he'd seen flit across Abby's features.

''What...? Ah...no,'' she responded, silently wondering how long it would be before Mitch uncovered the truth. ''I forgot to give your father a piece of bread with his dinner,'' she quickly improvised.

''I'll take it up, Mom.'' Toby started to climb down from his chair.

''That's all right, darling,'' Abby replied. ''I'm sure Mr. Tom won't mind for once.'' She managed a weak smile as she sat down at the table.

Throughout the meal Mitch chatted with Toby, asking the boy about his day at school. Abby watched with silent admiration as Mitch, with easy charm, lured Toby further and further out of his shell.

''You said you worked with my...dad,'' Toby began tentatively. ''That means you're a policeman, too. Right?''

Abby felt her stomach muscles tighten at the dangerous direction the conversation had taken.

''Yes,'' Mitch replied. ''Your father and I went through basic training together,'' he explained.

Abby threw Mitch a startled glance. Cal had led her to believe he and Mitch hadn't known each other well, that they'd only met while working at the police headquarters in Vancouver.

"What's basic training?" Toby asked, cutting into her thoughts.

"It's a lot like going to school," Mitch explained. "But instead of learning how to read and write like you do at your school, we learned about the law, about how to deal with criminals, how to arrest them, what to do at a crime scene, all kinds of things." He came to a halt. "Your dad must have told you all this already."

Toby shook his head. "He never—"

"Cal didn't talk much about work." Abby quickly cut in, fearful Toby might say something *she* would regret.

Mitch eyed her curiously, wondering at the look of panic he'd seen flash briefly in the depths of her green eyes.

"Do you have a uniform and a gun?" Toby continued, obviously eager to hear more about being a policeman.

"I have a gun, but I don't wear a uniform."

"You don't? Why not?" Toby wanted to know.

"Because I work undercover most of the time," Mitch explained, beginning to feel a bit worn out by Toby's barrage of questions.

"Undercover—is that like being a spy?" Toby asked, his blue eyes widening with interest.

Mitch nodded. "You could say that."

"Who do you spy on?" Toby asked.

"Criminals mostly," Mitch replied with a teasing grin, thinking the comments he'd heard about a child's unending curiosity were definitely true.

"Is it exciting? Do you ever get scared?" the boy asked, his gaze intent.

"It can be exciting. And yes, it often gets scary," Mitch replied, his right hand moving automatically to his left side in a protective gesture.

"Is it like you see in the movies?" Toby asked.

"No, it's not like the movies," Mitch answered with a smile. "I suppose you want to be a policeman like your father when you grow up," he commented, thinking that was the reason behind Toby's relentless questions.

But at his words, Toby's animated expression underwent a dramatic change. The eagerness and enthusiasm on the boy's face vanished like a newly melted snowflake, replaced by a guarded and rather sad look that tugged strangely at his heart.

"Toby, darling." Abby leapt in, attempting to cover Toby's sudden quietness. "Would you run upstairs and see if Mr. Tom needs anything?" she asked, all the while aware of Mitch's eyes on her.

Toby pushed his plate away and slid down from his chair.

"I'm sorry, I didn't mean to upset him," Mitch said the moment Toby had left the room. "I guess he still misses his father."

Abby had to clamp down on the bubble of hysterical laughter that suddenly threatened to burst free. "He'll be all right," Abby said. She got to her feet and gathered her own and Toby's dishes, then carried them to the sink.

Mitch rose and, picking up his own plate, followed Abby. "Toby's a great kid. Cal must have been very proud of his son," he remarked.

Abby was glad she had her back to Mitch as feelings of anger washed over her at the memory of how Cal had ignored Toby. She couldn't respond, refusing to acknowledge in any way an emotion Cal had neither felt nor expressed.

Suddenly they both heard a crash from the floor above. "Uh-oh. Sounds like Toby might need a hand," Abby said, and before Mitch could even react she was already halfway to the door.

Mitch stared after Abby in silence. He'd noted the tension in her shoulders moments before she'd made her escape and suspected that talking about her husband was a painful subject for Abby, too, and an indication of just how much she'd loved Cal... still loved him.

He sighed and ran a hand through his hair, recalling with startling clarity the smug look on Cal's face the day he'd stopped at Mitch's desk in the squad room and announced he was getting married to a nurse he'd been dating, a nurse named Abby Davidson.

Mitch had been hard-pressed to hide the shock that had spiraled through him at the news. He'd been planning on paying Abby a visit himself, that morning. But as was his habit he'd come into the office early to hand in his report on the undercover operation he'd just completed; an operation that had lasted more than three months, an operation he'd jeopardized the night he'd visited his mother in hospital, the night he'd spent a few magical and unforgettable hours in Abby's arms.

Not for the first time Mitch reminded himself that those hours he'd spent with Abby had meant nothing to her. She'd taken pity on him, sympathizing with his loss and offering comfort in the form of sex.

He'd thought something special had happened between them that night, but a few months later Abby had married another man. What surprised and disturbed him, however, was the discovery that even after seven years he should still feel such a deep sense of betrayal.

Chapter Five

Abby awoke with a start the next morning when Toby came bouncing into her room and onto her bed.

"Mom! Mom! You have to look outside," he said, his face alight with excitement. "You won't believe it."

"I won't believe what?" Abby responded teasingly, guessing Toby was referring to the amount of snow that had fallen during the night.

"It looks like the North Pole. It's so white and bright. Everything is buried in snow," he hurried on, a hint of wonder in his voice as he hopped off her bed and crossed to the window. "Quick! Come and see," he urged, beckoning her to join him, obviously fearful the snow would vanish before she had a chance to see it.

Abby smiled as she pushed the covers aside and padded across the carpeted floor to the window. As her gaze traveled outside, her mouth opened in astonishment when she saw the thick blanket of snow spreading as far as the eye could see.

"Wow!" It was all she could think of to say. She couldn't remember ever seeing so much snow before.

"Isn't it neat?" Toby said. "There won't be school today, will there? I mean, Mrs. Mac won't be able to drive the bus in the snow, will she?'' He glanced at her, a hopeful expression on his face.

''I doubt very much if even a snowplow could make it through today,'' Abby replied. ''We'll listen to the radio. If the school is closed they'll announce it on the radio. Dress warmly,'' she ordered as he scampered off to his room.

Abby shivered and rubbed her bare shoulders as she turned to gaze outside once more. Every twig on every branch of every tree was covered in a layer of snow and Abby stood mesmerized by the unspoiled beauty of the landscape before her.

The sky was cloud free and as blue as a bright summer's morning. Nothing stirred, not a wild creature, human or machine and Abby gazed in awe at the shimmering brilliance, finding the hushed silence infinitely soothing.

Her thoughts drifted back to the previous evening and the rather abrupt conclusion to the conversation at the dinner table. Since moving to Peachville she'd made a point of never talking about Cal, a subject that tended to upset Toby. Mitch's comment about Toby wanting to be like Cal had immediately resulted in the child's withdrawal, a reaction Mitch had interpreted as that of a boy still grieving over the loss of his father... which was a far cry from the truth.

Cal, who had professed to love her unborn child and accept it as his own, had for the most part ignored Toby from the time he was born. A bright and intelligent boy, Toby had soon realized that he would receive no love or affection from the man who lived in the apartment with him and his mother.

Though Cal never yelled at or physically abused her son, by deliberately withholding those emotions every child needs and deserves, he was cruelly leaving scars, emotional scars that were much more difficult to heal.

While Abby had shielded Toby from Cal's indifference as much as possible throughout the four years she had stayed with Cal, Toby had been without a positive male influence in his life, without a father figure who would guide and encourage him and give him support.

Toby had known Cal was a policeman, but while he might have been curious about the profession, he'd also known better than to voice a comment or ask a question.

In contrast, Mitch was much more approachable. His natural warmth and easy charm had quickly made inroads into Toby's usual reserve, winning him over with an ease that Abby found surprising, until she reminded herself that Mitch was Toby's natural father, a fact that could readily account for the rapport between them.

Should she simply tell Mitch the truth? It was a question that had kept her awake well into the night. How would he react? What would he do? she wondered for the hundredth time.

"Mom, the light in my closet isn't working," Toby said, breaking into Abby's thoughts.

"That's because the power is out." The comment came from Mitch, and at the sound of his deep, resonant voice Abby spun around. Mitch, dressed in jeans and black pullover sweater, stood gazing at her from the bedroom doorway.

Abby felt her heart kick against her rib cage at the sight of him, and as their glances collided, an emotion she couldn't decipher flashed briefly in the depths of his eyes.

"Mom, aren't you getting dressed?" Toby asked, and at his words Abby felt a rush of heat suffuse her face at the realization that all she was wearing was her pink sheer nightdress.

"The furnace is out. I'm going to light the fire in the living room," Mitch said, noting her flushed cheeks. "Dad usually keeps it primed and ready to go at this time of year." His gaze lingered for a moment on the rapid rise and fall of her chest. "If the power isn't back on soon, the house will slowly lose heat. A fire will help take the edge off the chill," he went on, though the sight of Abby in a sexy nightdress was effectively igniting a heat of a much more personal nature. "I'd better check the wood pile, too, but if I know my father, there'll be more than enough."

"Can I help carry in some wood?" Toby asked.

"You sure can," Mitch replied, smiling down at the boy's eager expression. "Come on, let's get the show on the road."

As Toby followed Mitch down the hall, Abby crossed to close her bedroom door, leaning against it momentarily for support. Beneath her nightdress her body tingled with awareness, aroused by the heated look she'd seen in Mitch's eyes.

Annoyed at herself and her unwanted reaction, Abby dressed and a few minutes later knocked on Tom's bedroom door.

"Good morning, Tom," she said brightly.

"Morning, Abby," Tom responded. "I gather we have a power outage."

"Yes, we do," Abby confirmed. "Mitch has gone downstairs to light the fire in the living room," she told him.

"Good idea," Tom acknowledged. "There's lots of wood. I had a cord delivered and stacked last month. It's dry and ready to go."

Abby smiled. "Mitch thought you'd probably have everything in hand," she remarked.

"Did he, now," Tom responded, a glint of satisfaction in his eyes. "Well, he's right. I always keep the woodpile stocked, especially at this time of year. How much snow did we get?"

"Close to three feet, I'd say," Abby told him.

"Ah-ha! My bunion was right!" Tom announced gleefully. "That's what I predicted," he added with a chortle.

Abby smiled. "You should get it patented," she teased as she straightened his quilt. "Are you warm enough? Shall I get you another blanket?"

"I'm fine," he assured her. "Snug as a bug in a rug." He grinned.

"I'll go and put the kettle on...." She stopped and grinned sheepishly. "On second thought, that's out of the question," she commented, remembering there was no electricity. "I don't suppose you have a camp stove?"

"I do, as a matter of fact," Tom replied. "We did a lot of camping in the old days. It hasn't been used in quite some time, though, but you should find it in the pantry somewhere. Try the top shelf," he suggested. "The darn thing can be a bit tricky to get going, but Mitch can give you a hand, if you have trouble."

"Thanks, but I'm sure I can manage," Abby said confidently, determined not to ask Mitch for help. Having him around was bad enough. His very presence created havoc with her senses and compounded the fear that he might at any moment discover the truth about Toby's true parentage.

Downstairs, near the back porch, Abby opened the pantry door and automatically reached inside for the light switch, muttering under her breath at her own stupidity when nothing happened.

How on earth was she supposed to find the camp stove in the dark? Taking a tentative step inside, she peered at the dark shelves stocked with various items—canned foods, empty mason jars, dry goods and other odds and ends. What she really needed was a flashlight. She should have asked Tom where they were kept. And candles, too, for that matter. If the power outage lasted all day, they'd need candles later.

"Need a hand?"

Abby's heart did a quick flip at the sound of Mitch's voice coming from directly behind her. She turned, and her pulse instantly picked up speed when she saw his silhouetted figure filling the doorway.

"Ah...your father said there's a camp stove in here," she told him.

"That's right, there is," Mitch replied easily. "And there should be a couple of flashlights somewhere...and candles, too," he added. "My mother was a very practical person—she liked to have a place for everything and everything in its place. She always kept a metal box with candles and matches on the lower shelf, just for emergencies. It's my guess it's still there. The lower shelf, on your left."

Mitch took another step into the narrow pantry. His broad shoulders and tall bearing blocked out what little daylight there was, and for the first time in her life Abby understood what it meant to be claustrophobic.

"My left?" she managed to say, her voice husky and wavering slightly, wishing with quiet intensity that the power would miraculously come back on and illuminate the pantry.

"Yes...here," Mitch said. As he reached past her to the shelf beyond, his arm accidentally brushed against her breasts, sending a bolt of heat racing to the center of her being. Abby sucked in her breath at the searing contact as her nipple hardened in instant arousal.

Tiny sparks of sensation darted across her nerve endings, spreading the heat in ever-widening circles until her whole body quivered with a longing she'd never thought to feel again. Suddenly Abby was glad of the darkness, glad that Mitch couldn't see her reaction as she fought to regain control of senses gone dangerously awry.

"Here it is!" Mitch announced, easing his body away from hers.

Seconds later Abby felt the cold touch of metal against her hands and with trembling fingers she took the tin from him, hugging it against her chest like a protective shield.

"If my memory serves me well, the flashlights are on the shelf below," Mitch said as he moved toward her again.

Abby instinctively took a step back, anxious to avoid any further contact with Mitch. "I'll get out of your way," she said a trifle breathlessly before deftly sidestepping him and making her escape.

The sudden brightness of the porch dazzled her for a moment, but, intent on putting as much distance between herself and Mitch as possible, Abby headed for the relative safety of the kitchen. She stood for several moments clutching the metal container, still reeling from the encounter in the pantry.

It wasn't fair that with one brief touch Mitch could set her on fire. But, she reminded herself, that's exactly how things had gotten so quickly out of hand seven years ago. All he'd done that night was kiss her. A simple kiss. A thank-you kiss. But the second their lips had met everything had changed. Desire, hot and needy, as powerful and unstoppable as a tornado, had spun them out of control.

"Mom? Oh! There you are," Toby said as he came running into the kitchen. "I was looking for you upstairs. I can't find my boots."

Abby deliberately clamped down on the memories threatening to overwhelm her. "They're in the laundry room," she managed to say, hoping Toby wouldn't notice her distress. To her relief he ran down the hallway past the pantry to the laundry room.

"I found the flashlights and the camp stove," Mitch said a few moments later when he joined her in the kitchen. "I should have looked these out last night when we still had power."

Abby drew a steadying breath. "When do you think the work crews will have the power restored?" she asked, keeping her tone even.

"It's hard to predict," came the reply. "Do you need a hand getting this thing started?" he asked, setting the camp stove on the counter and flipping open the top. "It doesn't look like it's been used in ages and it's tricky if you've never done it before."

"Thanks, but I'm sure I can figure it out," Abby replied, more determined than ever to get the stove going on her own, although as she gazed at it, the idea of cooking anything on a tiny gas burner—never mind breakfast for four—suddenly seemed a rather daunting prospect.

"I'm ready!" The shout came from Toby, who appeared from the hallway wearing his jacket and toque, boots and gloves.

"Be right with you," Mitch said with a smile. "Toby and I are going to dig a path to the woodpile then haul in as much wood as the firewood box in the laundry room will hold," Mitch went on. "I lit the fire in the living room, and as long as we keep throwing on logs, the house should stay reasonably warm."

"I'll see if I can rustle up some tea and toast," she offered.

"Good idea," Mitch replied before turning to follow Toby to the back door.

* * *

The power outage lasted for most of the day. To Abby's delight she mastered the camp stove and found the challenge of using only one burner to make tea and toast, as well as warm up soup for lunch, not as difficult as she'd anticipated.

From his bedroom Toby monitored the radio bulletins, which confirmed the school closure and told of impassable road conditions and downed telephone and electric wires throughout the area.

When power was finally restored late in the afternoon, Abby busied herself baking several meat-and-vegetable pies as well as a large pot of beef stew, which, in the event of a second power outage, could easily be reheated on the camp stove.

Toby followed Mitch around for most of the day, occasionally running back and forth from Tom's bedroom, giving updates on the weather and being Mitch's general helper. He even built a snowman, with Mitch's help, but not before they'd cleared a second path from the front door to the truck.

Ever since she'd been trapped for those heart-stopping moments in the pantry with Mitch, Abby had made a concentrated effort never to be alone with him. And she'd succeeded, thanks to Toby, who appeared to have developed a case of hero-worship for the man who was his father.

For the next two days the snowstorm kept them housebound, but nobody, especially not Toby, who spent every waking minute with Mitch, seemed to mind in the least.

Watching Toby interact with his father brought an ache to Abby's heart, but she couldn't bring herself to discipline or reprimand him, not when for the first time in his young life he was being given positive reinforcement and encouragement, and Mitch didn't appear to mind the fact that he'd acquired a pint-size shadow.

Abby tried to tell herself that once the roads were cleared and school was reconvened, Toby would revert to his old patterns. But somewhere deep inside she knew she was only fooling herself, and the bond slowly being forged between

Toby and the man who was his father would have a lasting effect on her son.

"Hurry and put your coat and boots on, Toby. The school bus will be here any minute," Abby said on the first day school began again.

"Bye, Mitch!" Toby called as Abby tied her son's scarf around his neck.

"See you later, squirt," Mitch replied from the upstairs landing as Toby hurried outside and down the snow-covered driveway.

Abby closed the door and made her way back to the kitchen.

"Oh...Abby..."

Abby slowed to a halt and glanced at Mitch as he descended the stairs. His hair, still slightly damp, looked like polished ebony, and she noted that the lines of strain around his mouth and eyes had disappeared. Dressed in hip-hugging blue jeans and a long-sleeved white polo-necked shirt, he looked incredibly attractive, and Abby felt her heart kick wildly in a response she couldn't control.

"I'm going into town to see how things are at the store," he said. "Is there anything you need?"

Abby moistened lips that were dry. "Ah...milk. We've all been drinking our share of hot chocolate these past few days," she said. "Oh, and maybe some extra flashlight batteries, just in case," she told him, silently wishing her pulse would slow down. She could smell the woodsy fragrance of his after-shave mingled with the clean male scent of him, a dangerous combination that set her nerves ajitter.

"I think I can remember that," Mitch replied easily. "I'll see you later." Crossing to the coat stand, he removed his parka and headed for the door.

As Mitch sat in his truck waiting for the engine to warm up, he found his thoughts drifting over the past few days when they'd all been prisoners of the storm. It was a situation he was accustomed to, having spent countless assignments holed up in a grubby hotel room waiting for something to happen.

But this had been totally different, because during the past few days he'd experienced a feeling of contentment and a sense of peace he hadn't known in a long time.

His body was slowly healing, and his strength was steadily returning. But what he found most surprising was the fact that the tension and stress that had forever been a constant in his life had noticeably diminished, as if a weight had magically been lifted from his shoulders.

The demands made on him here were decidedly simple and unencumbered by the worry of having to be always on guard and alert to every possible danger. And his father, though still not openly communicative, was beginning to show signs of warming up to having him home.

And, of course, there was Toby. He'd found the boy's innate sense of fun and joy of life infectious and heart-warming, and he'd realized with a pang that somewhere along the way he'd forgotten the art of delighting in life's simple pleasures.

With Toby's help he'd kept the wood box in the laundry room well stocked, and he and Toby had had a wonderful time building a monstrous snowman to stand guard near the woodpile.

He felt inexorably drawn to the boy, who reminded him of how he himself had been at that age; a youth with the same healthy curiosity and willingness to learn, mixed with a keen intelligence and an eagerness to please.

That he'd forged a bond with Toby came as something of a surprise for Mitch, especially when Toby's father had been one of the few men in his life Mitch had truly disliked.

From the first day of basic training, Cal Roberts had had a chip on his shoulder, constantly striving to prove to anyone and everyone he was the best. But he hadn't been the best, not in the field or in the classroom. Mitch had captured that honor. As a result, a rivalry had sprung up between them, a rivalry that had appeared friendly, at least on the outside.

By the end of basic training Mitch had topped the class, with Cal a distant second, and after the results were announced Mitch had been hard-pressed to ignore Cal's open bitterness and animosity. Less than a week later, Mitch had been recruited by the head of undercover operations and it had been over four years before he'd seen Cal again.

Though Cal had greeted him with a smile and a handshake, Mitch hadn't been fooled, sensing the same underlying bitterness, the same feelings of resentment Cal had exhibited during their days in basic training.

Working in different departments, and with Mitch's assignments taking him away sometimes for months at a time, their paths hadn't crossed much, and Mitch could only wonder if he would have accepted Abby's offer of a cup of coffee and a shoulder to cry on that night so long ago had he known she was involved with Cal.

But he hadn't known and Abby hadn't bothered to enlighten him. She'd felt sorry for him, nothing more, and he was a romantic fool to have thought anything else. Added to that had been the rumor that started circulating, hinting that Abby had always been free with her favors.

Mitch grimaced in self-reproach. She'd played him for a fool. Plain and simple. And if the rumors were true he wasn't the first man to be taken in by her sympathetic smile and her warm body. Annoyed at the route his thoughts had taken, he quickly put the truck in gear and headed down the driveway.

"Will Mitch be home soon?" Toby asked for the third time in the past half hour.

Abby sighed as she grated cheese on top of the macaroni casserole she'd removed from the oven. Toby had been home for several hours, but after finishing his homework he'd been wearing down a path from the kitchen to the front door.

Abby glanced at the clock. It was past five and quite dark outside. "He'll be—" she began, but the sound of the front door opening brought her to a halt.

Toby immediately hopped down from the kitchen chair and raced for the door.

"Hey, buddy. How was your day at school?" Abby heard Mitch greet Toby and felt her eyes sting with tears at the warmth and affection she could hear in his voice. Hurriedly she blinked away the moisture and, putting on her oven gloves, picked up the casserole and carried it back to the oven for the final stages of cooking.

"Hmm...that looks scrumptious," Mitch commented as he entered. "But what's everyone else having? There's barely enough there for me," he said in a teasing tone, flashing a cheeky grin at Abby before closing the oven door for her.

Abby quickly controlled the shiver that danced across her skin in reaction to his grin, but she couldn't resist the twinkle in his eyes or the playfulness she heard in his voice.

"Oh, sir, I beg you..." Abby spoke in her best Scarlett O'Hara drawl. "I'm not hungry. But if you could but spare my son a few mouthfuls..." She clasped her oven-gloved hands together at her breast in an affected and exaggerated pose. "Why, he's only a child, sir," she continued, ending with a loud and realistic sob.

"Mom!" Toby gazed in astonishment at his mother, obviously embarrassed by her display. "Mitch was only kidding," he told her.

"Ah...Scarlett...I mean, your mother is, too," Mitch told Toby, his smile widening to encompass both mother and son.

"Oh, Mom..." Toby said in a beleaguered tone.

Abby glanced at Mitch and suddenly they were laughing. The deep, rich sound filled the kitchen and a new and different warmth enfolded them as Toby joined in. It had been a long time since she'd laughed out loud with such carefree abandon, but then, there hadn't been too much in her life to laugh about.

"Who's Scarlett?" Toby asked a few moments later, sending Mitch and Abby into fresh gales of laughter. "You guys are silly," Toby announced, peeved at the way the adults were behaving.

"Yes, I suppose we are," Mitch acknowledged, still smiling. "But laughter is good for the soul," he observed, stirred more than he was willing to admit by the spark he could see in the depths of her green eyes.

He had forgotten how intimate, how sensuous a shared moment like this could be, and he was having difficulty curbing the impulse to gather Abby into his arms and spin her around the floor.

"Want to play a game of checkers?" Toby asked, cutting through Mitch's wayward thoughts.

"I thought I'd pop upstairs and see my father. He's probably anxious to hear how things went at the store today," Mitch said, and saw a look of disappointment cross Toby's features. "How about we play a game or two after supper?" Mitch suggested.

"Okay." Toby instantly brightened.

True to his word, after supper Mitch followed Toby to the living room, where he'd already set up the board game. After retrieving Tom's tray from his bedroom, Abby washed the dishes, lingering in the kitchen even after she was finished, listening to the occasional moan or groan from Mitch or a shout of triumph from Toby.

"I suppose it's too late to ask if you need any help."

Abby, who'd been watering a small ivy plant on the windowsill, jumped at the sound of Mitch's voice. "I thought you were playing checkers," she said as she set the watering can on the counter, trying to ignore the ripple of awareness chasing down her spine.

"I was," Mitch replied. "But Toby suddenly remembered a Christmas special on television tonight he wanted to watch," Mitch explained.

"Oh, I see," Abby replied.

"I came to ask a favor," Mitch said.

"A favor?" Abby repeated, surprised and faintly alarmed as she met his gaze.

"My stitches have been bothering me all day," he told her. "I'm not sure if it's the dressing itself or the tape that's causing the problem. I was wondering if you'd mind taking a look."

Abby's heart beat frantically in response to the request. "Sure," she managed to say. "I'll just get the first aid kit," she added, relieved that she would have a few moments to prepare herself. "I'll be right back."

When Abby returned with the first aid kit, Mitch had removed his sweater. Her heart gave a quick, unsteady leap at the sight of his lean, muscular back and she was unprepared for the sweet rush of desire that suddenly swamped her. Angry at her own weakness, Abby gritted her teeth and resolutely clamped down on her errant emotions.

Mitch turned to see Abby, her face expressionless, cross to the table. "The dressing came off," Mitch said, glancing down at the wound on his side. "I had trouble keeping it dry in the shower this morning," he added.

At his words an image of Mitch, naked in the shower, flashed into Abby's mind, sending her heart into a tailspin. With hands that weren't quite steady, Abby set the first aid box on the table, fighting to maintain a professional manner.

"Looks like it's healing nicely," she said as she glanced at the wound. "These dissolving stitches can sometimes pull a bit." Abby removed a small pair of scissors from the kit. With practiced ease she snipped away several loose strands of thread. "That should take care of it," she said a moment later.

Mitch slowly released the breath he'd been holding, amazed that he'd hardly felt a thing, so gentle was her touch. "Thanks," he murmured.

As he gazed down at her bent head, the familiar scent of lemons mixed with the erotic fragrance of lilacs assaulted his senses and it was all he could do not to reach out and capture her hair and run his hands through its silky softness.

"I'll put on a fresh dressing," Abby said. "A large Band-Aid should be sufficient now."

Abby drew a ragged breath as she removed the package from the first aid box. Mitch's nearness was slowly and insidiously playing havoc with her resolve to remain detached. Her fingers itched to explore the broad planes of his chest, to trace the outline of his ribs and feel the heated smoothness of his skin. With hands that were trembling she fumbled with the package, all the while fighting to ignore the longing tugging at her heart.

"Here, let me do that," Mitch offered.

As he reached for the package, his knuckles brushed against Abby's, sending a jolt of electricity up her arm. At the searing contact Abby lost her hold on the package and it slid from her grasp to fall to the floor.

Mitch and Abby each bent to retrieve the package at the same time, an action that resulted in a collision of heads.

"Sorry, Abby. Are you all right?" Mitch asked, concern in his voice as he grasped her upper arms to steady her.

"Yes…I think so," Abby replied a little breathlessly, her forehead throbbing from the contact. She felt a little dazed, but as she lifted her eyes to meet his, she was almost sure the dizziness besieging her had nothing to do with the collision and everything to do with the fact that Mitch's face was a scant two inches from her own.

His warm breath gently caressed her face and Abby felt her heart leap into her throat as his eyes, intense and very focused, seemed to be trying to see inside her soul. Slowly, achingly, tantalizingly he closed the gap between them as if drawn by an invisible force.

As their mouths met and melded, Abby surrendered to the sweet sensations his kiss evoked. A dark dusky heat began to spread through her, igniting a need she'd almost forgotten how to feel.

With hands that were trembling she caressed the taut muscles of his upper arms, reveling in the feel of his skin as she slowly traversed the smooth curve of his shoulders and neck until her fingers buried themselves in the springy softness of his hair to urge him closer.

Mitch crushed her to him and she could feel his arousal pressing insistently against her abdomen, which only served to fan the flames of her desire. As his tongue invaded, demanded and devoured, she gloried in the passion she could taste on his lips, a passion that nearly matched her own. The moan came from somewhere deep in her throat as her body melted against his like candle wax touched by flame.

Mitch heard the soft, shaky sound vibrating in Abby's throat and felt his heart kick against his rib cage in wild response as a desire strong and powerful vibrated through him, igniting a need he'd felt only once before.

He'd forgotten the intense thrill of holding her in his arms, forgotten how her whole body quivered in fiery response to his kiss, forgotten how the soft sound of her sigh and the sweet scent of her skin could inflame his senses and demolish his control.

He'd burned for her that night seven years ago and he was burning for her now as the exotic taste of her and the sensual feel of her body pressed against his drove him perilously close to the edge.

"Mom? Mom?"

Through the haze of passion threatening to consume her, Abby heard Toby's voice, and the sound had the effect of a splash of ice-cold water. Abby broke free of Mitch's embrace, spinning away from him in an action that was partly self-preservation, partly reflex. She was fighting for breath, furious with herself at the way she'd succumbed so eagerly to his kiss, a kiss whose aftereffects were still thrumming through her system, making it difficult for her to even think straight.

"The show's over," Toby said. "What are you guys doing?" He came to a halt at the sight of the first aid kit on the table. "What happened?" The boy's attention was riveted on the ugly red scar on Mitch's side.

"I had an accident," Mitch said, managing to keep his tone even, as he struggled to extinguish the fire raging through him.

"An accident?" Toby repeated, his eyes widening in surprise. "Where? At the store?" he asked.

"No," Mitch replied, wondering how best to explain the knife wound.

"I was putting a clean bandage on the wound," Abby said, bending to retrieve the one she'd dropped.

Toby stared at Mitch's jagged scar. "You've got stitches," he noted, glancing up at Mitch.

"That's right," Mitch acknowledged as Abby proceeded to complete what she'd set out to do earlier.

"Did you get shot?" Toby suddenly asked, and Mitch glimpsed the flicker of fear in the depths of the boy's eyes. "Are you going to die?"

"No, Toby, I'm not going to die," Mitch assured him, touched by the concern he'd heard in Toby's voice. "It's only a knife wound," Mitch added, suddenly glad of

Toby's questions, which helped to divert his attention from Abby's gentle ministerings.

"Ca—my father got shot. And he died," Toby said matter-of-factly.

"I know," Mitch said. "I'm sorry, Toby. Believe me, I know how hard it is to lose someone you love." He wished there was something more he could say that would ease the boy's pain.

Toby lifted his gaze to meet Mitch's. "But I didn't—"

"Toby!" Abby quickly cut in before her son could finish, almost positive Toby had been about to say that he didn't love his father. "Isn't it time for your bath?" she asked, pinning a bright smile on her face, all the while aware of Mitch's frowning gaze. "Come on. Let's go!" Gathering up the first aid kit, she put her hand on Toby's shoulder and gently urged him from the room.

"Night, Mitch," Toby said over his shoulder.

"Night, sport," Mitch replied as he reached for his sweater and pulled it on. He stood for several moments wondering at the flash of panic he'd seen in Abby's eyes before she'd cut Toby off in midsentence. Any mention of Cal seemed to generate the same response from Abby, and Mitch was at a loss to know why.

But what disturbed him by far was the kiss they'd shared. Silently he berated himself for letting it happen, but he'd been unable to resist, drawn like a man dying of thirst to the water that would revive him.

He'd wanted her with an intensity that shocked him, and though he knew he was a fool, he also knew that from the moment he'd walked in and found her in his father's house she'd posed a danger to his heart, an even bigger danger than the knife-wielding assailant he'd fought off on the streets of Toronto.

But he'd trusted his heart to her once before and suffered the consequences, and he'd be foolish indeed to fall under her spell a second time.

Chapter Six

As Abby followed her son upstairs she breathed a sigh of relief at having managed to forestall Toby from revealing his true feelings about Cal. Abby knew she was fortunate, in view of the relationship that had blossomed between Toby and Mitch, that Toby hadn't already voiced his dislike of the man everyone believed was his father.

She wasn't altogether sure why she felt the need to keep this aspect of Cal secret, other than her own guilt and shame at allowing him to manipulate her for his own twisted and obscure reasons. She would always regret their marriage, always regret the pain she'd subjected Toby to simply because she'd had nowhere else to go and no one else to turn to.

Leaving Toby playing happily in the bathtub, Abby heard the low murmur of voices coming from behind Tom's bedroom door, telling her that Mitch had joined his father. Relieved not to have to face him again, she returned to the kitchen to prepare a bedtime snack for Toby.

As she waited for the mug of milk to heat in the microwave she kept on the alert for the sound of Mitch's return. Stirring the chocolate powder into the warm milk, she let her thoughts return to those unforgettable moments when she'd found herself wrapped in his arms, responding with a wantonness that even now brought a blush to her cheeks and a shiver of renewed awareness chasing down her spine.

What was there about Mitch that set her soul on fire? Even after seven years the sexual chemistry that erupted between them was as volatile now as it had been then. But resolutely she reminded herself that chemistry wasn't everything. She was older now and a good deal wiser, and while her body might respond to Mitch, welcoming him like a long-lost lover, she was determined he'd never again touch her heart.

Seven years ago she'd been totally innocent and completely unskilled in the art of making love. Not that she hadn't had her share of boyfriends. But she'd been too intent on getting the grades required to get into the nurses' training program to spend too much time dating.

The young men she had gone out with had been much more interested in introducing her to the physical side of a relationship than in getting to know her, and she'd soon tired of their awkward groping and murmured insistence that everyone was doing it. Consequently she'd shied away from relationships, unwilling to indulge in sex just for the sake of finding out what the hoopla was all about.

She'd met Cal in the hospital emergency room on a sunny afternoon when he'd brought in a young man with facial cuts and a broken arm. She'd often wondered if the reason she'd accepted Cal's invitation to go out on a date was that, dressed in his police uniform, he'd reminded her a little of Mitch.

They'd spent a pleasant evening, which had ended with a brief but enjoyable good-night kiss. He'd called her again and they'd gone bowling. When he'd called her a third time she'd had to decline, explaining that her shifts at the hospital had been changed, making it difficult for her to plan a social life.

It had been less than a week later that she'd run into Mitch wandering aimlessly through the hospital corridors. At first he'd been so wrapped up in his grief that he hadn't recognized her, but when she introduced herself he'd seemed relieved to see a friendly face. When he'd told her about his mother, Abby hadn't had the heart or the will-power to just walk away.

He hadn't protested when she'd suggested what he needed was a good strong cup of coffee, but with the hospital cafeteria located on the other side of the building, Abby had decided that her apartment was much closer and more convenient.

Mitch had been silent during the short walk, but once inside her apartment he'd asked questions about her job and whether or not she liked living in Vancouver, talking about anything and everything but what was really on his mind. Over coffee the conversation had turned to Peachville and they'd chatted about mutual acquaintances until they'd finally exhausted those subjects, too.

When he'd risen to leave, she'd found herself wishing fervently that their meeting had happened under better circumstances. He'd thanked her for the coffee and for her kindness and impulsively she'd reached up to touch his cheek in a gesture of pure and sincere sympathy. He'd captured her hand in his and, equally impulsively, he'd leaned forward to gently brush her lips in a kiss simply meant as a thank-you.

But the moment their mouths touched everything had changed, and all at once the world had exploded around them, spinning them out of control and into a vortex of passion impossible to escape, even if they'd wanted to.

The sound of a door slamming somewhere upstairs brought Abby instantly out of her reverie and back to the present. She shivered and muttered under her breath at the realization that the milk in the mug had begun to cool.

Pressing the timer on the microwave, she quickly re-heated the milk, all the while thinking that she'd given Mitch her heart and soul that night, responding to *his* kiss, *his* touch, *his* needs, trustingly going wherever he led, until she'd lost herself in the wonder of his arms.

But he'd walked out of her life without a backward glance and she had no reason to believe, if she was foolish enough to be seduced a second time, that he wouldn't simply walk away again.

Abby hurried upstairs with the mug of hot chocolate, past Tom's room and into Toby's, to find her son in his pajamas, sitting up in bed.

"Did you bring me a cookie, too?" Toby asked as Abby crossed to set the mug on the small bedside table.

"Did you let the water out of the tub?" she countered, keeping the cookie hidden behind her back.

Toby shook his head and scrunched up his face in an apologetic plea, breaking instantly into a smile when she brought his cookie out of hiding.

"Thanks, Mom," he said. "You're the greatest," he added with a sheepish grin.

Abby smiled, too. "Oh, you charmer you, just like you—" She stopped abruptly, the smile evaporating as she smothered the words "your father." She'd been thinking of Mitch, but Toby wouldn't know that and she'd have upset him had she made the reference that he was in any way like Cal.

"Just like what, Mom?" Toby asked, looking up at her with a puzzled frown.

"Ah...just like you to forget to drain the tub," she quickly improvised, forcing herself to smile once more.

Toby's frown disappeared at her words. "Will you read me a story?" he asked as he popped the remainder of the cookie into his mouth.

"Oh, I guess I could," she said with pretended reluctance.

Half an hour later, after Toby had brushed his teeth and she'd kissed him good-night, Abby quietly closed her son's bedroom door and headed downstairs. Passing Tom's room, she wondered if Mitch was still with his father, but this time she could hear no sounds coming from inside.

As she entered the kitchen she came to a halt at the sight of Mitch sitting at the table, his hands curled around a mug.

"Is Toby asleep?" Mitch asked, glancing around at her.

"Almost," Abby replied as she moved to the sink to rinse Toby's mug.

"I made a pot of tea," Mitch said. "Why don't you join me?"

Abby's heart jolted against her breastbone at the invitation. Her first instinct was to decline, but gazing at Mitch's figure hunched at the table, at the thoughtful expression on his face, she hesitated.

The memory of the electrifying kiss they'd shared earlier still lingered. She knew she should leave, yet there was something about his demeanor, something that tugged strangely at her heartstrings.

Taking a mug from the cupboard, she half filled it from the teapot on the counter. "Is anything wrong?" she asked before taking a sip.

Mitch was silent for a long moment, making Abby wonder if he'd even heard her. She was about to repeat the question when he spoke. "I was upstairs trying to talk to my father. I thought it was time we sorted a few things out—" He broke off. "But he refuses to listen." He shook his head. Picking up the mug with both hands, he took a sip.

Abby, determined to keep her distance, leaned back against the counter. "Are there more problems at the store?" she asked, unsure what Mitch was referring to.

"No. That's one area we can talk about," he replied. "In fact, he talks at great length about what I should be doing at the store, or what I could be doing. He's even listened to and liked some of the ideas I've had about ways to improve things," he told her. "But the minute I bring up the subject of my mother, he clams up."

Abby tried to harden her heart against the pain she could hear in Mitch's voice. "Maybe he just needs more time," she ventured.

"Time! Damn it, Abby! It's been seven years. How much time does he need?" Mitch demanded, his blue eyes flashing with anger. "I'm sorry," he added, immediately contrite. "It's not your fault."

Abby shrugged. "If he hasn't talked about your mother in seven years, it's bound to be difficult for him. How long were they married?" she asked, thinking Mitch might feel better if he was able to talk to someone about his mother.

"She died a few months before their thirtieth wedding anniversary," Mitch replied with a sad smile. "Mom loved to celebrate birthdays and anniversaries. She even made up special days just so she could have something to celebrate. Like Construction Day." His smile widened at the memory. "That's the day the builders started work on the addition to the house. And of course, there was Completion Day when the work was finished and my mother and father finally moved in to what she liked to call their dream bedroom." He was silent for a moment. "She sure loved that room," he went on. "She was proud of the fact that she chose the colors and did all the decorating herself. She picked the fabrics and most of the furniture. She just had a great time putting it all together."

"Oh...so that's why..." Abby mumbled, almost to herself.

"That's why what?" Mitch asked, glancing at her with curiosity.

Forgetting her resolve to keep her distance, Abby, mug in hand, crossed to sit down at the table with Mitch. "On the day your father was brought home from the hospital, I never understood why he insisted on being taken to the bedroom upstairs, especially when there was such a lovely room downstairs," she said.

"Your father had already given me his keys and I came ahead to open the house," she explained. "I took a quick look around and found the downstairs bedroom. The drapes were closed and the room looked like it hadn't been used in a long time, but it was on the main floor, and so much more convenient. I assumed that's where he'd go.

"But he'd have none of it," she went on. "He was adamant that he wanted to be taken upstairs. And that's where the attendants took him. After they left, he told me to stay out of that room, and to keep the door locked. He didn't say why and I didn't ask."

"I see," Mitch said solemnly. "He probably hasn't set foot in it since before my mother died," he added with a sigh.

"That's so sad," Abby replied. "And if he was on the main floor instead of upstairs, he could, with the help of a wheelchair, be having his meals with us."

"I guess the bedroom has too many memories of my mother," Mitch said, his tone sympathetic. "You know, when the doctors told us how ill she was, he refused to accept it. I don't remember ever seeing him as angry as he was then. He just couldn't understand how they could calmly tell him his wife was dying and do nothing to save her."

"That's really not an uncommon reaction," Abby answered softly.

"I know," Mitch responded. "He kept insisting they were wrong, and that he wanted another opinion. But there was nothing anyone could do." He sighed. "He drove her to other specialists, hoping one would tell him the original diagnosis was a mistake, that she was going to be fine. It was all futile."

Suddenly Mitch brought his fist down on the table. "Damn it! He should have brought her home to the house she loved, to the room she loved. This is where she wanted to be, not in a hospital."

Abby's heart ached for him and she reached over and covered his clenched fist with her hand. At the contact a shiver of sensation darted up her arm but she ignored it. "Mitch, don't! What good does this anger do you now?" she asked. "And as for your father, that was just his way of dealing with his," she told him gently.

Mitch lifted his eyes to meet hers. "I told him to take her home, to let her die in peace. And he accused me of not caring, of wanting my mother to die—" He broke off abruptly and closed his eyes.

Beneath her fingers Abby could feel the tension thrumming through him, vibrating like the string of an archer's bow, and she knew he was struggling to hold back tears.

"The week before she died I was working on an assignment and had been for nearly a month," Mitch went on, his voice husky, but in control. "Dad tried to track me down. He left several messages, urgent messages on my answering machine and with my supervisor at the department, to tell me Mom was at the hospital, that time was running out."

Pulling away from Abby, he sat back in his chair, spearing both hands through his hair in frustration and despair.

A lock of hair fell onto his forehead and Abby's fingers suddenly itched to comb it back in place, but steadfastly she fought the impulse.

"A day later I happened to call the department from a pay phone to check on something, and that's when I got the message. I immediately called the hospital but the woman on the switchboard would only tell me that my mother was resting comfortably. There was no way I could get hold of my father, and I had to go back to the job. I couldn't just drop everything and go over there.

"I can only imagine that my failure to get back to him, my failure to rush right over to the hospital, only confirmed that I didn't care. But, damn it, there was nothing I could do. The department was counting on me, and as it was the situation was extremely delicate and potentially volatile.

"If I broke my cover I ran the risk of jeopardizing the whole operation. All I could do was hope that we could wind things up quickly, but it wasn't to be. It took another two months before we finally nailed those guys—two whole months," he emphasized with a tired sigh.

Abby frowned and threw him a startled glance. "But you came to the hospital," she noted.

"Yes, I did," Mitch replied. "I couldn't stay away. I had to see my mother. And it almost cost me my job," he told her.

"Your job? But how?" Abby asked, trying with difficulty to sort out what Mitch had said.

"Because I was on an assignment, working undercover. I shouldn't have gone to the hospital. I almost blew the entire operation," he said. "But I had no choice, I had to take the chance. I grabbed a cab and told the driver to cruise around for a while. I wanted to make sure no one was following me. I finally got him to drop me outside the hospital around midnight.

"I found my mother's room and slipped inside, but Dad wasn't there. Mom looked like she was asleep and so I sat down and held her hand." His voice was husky with emotion and Abby felt tears prick her eyes as she listened.

"I kept expecting my father to walk in, but no one appeared, not even a nurse," Mitch said. "I must have been there twenty minutes when she opened her eyes." His voice was little more than a whisper now. "She was too weak to speak but she managed a smile, and just for a second I felt her hand gently squeeze mine. Then she let go." He stopped and was silent for a long time, his head bent in abject sorrow.

"She waited for you," Abby said, knowing he needed to hear it, and knowing from her experience as a nurse that patients who were terminally ill often managed to hold off death until they'd seen each family member.

Mitch lifted his gaze to meet hers. "Do you think so?"

Abby saw the glimmer of hope in his eyes and her heart melted. "I'm positive," she assured him and watched as his eyes closed for a moment in obvious relief.

"I went looking for my father...a nurse...anyone," Mitch suddenly continued. "I don't remember much of anything after that, until you found me. I'm not sure if I ever thanked you...."

Suddenly the air between them was crackling with tension and Abby rose from the chair and crossed to the sink, determined to hold on to her temper. There had been something almost insulting in the words he'd spoken, almost as if he was implying that he'd forgotten his manners and hadn't thanked her for sleeping with him.

"Abby, I'm sorry—"

"Don't be," she quickly retorted. "I took pity on you...remember? Your words, not mine," she added, deliberately choosing the phrase he'd used to describe their encounter, hoping to hurt him just as he'd hurt her. An unlikely event, she realized with a pang. In order to hurt his feelings he'd have to care.

"Look, I—" Mitch began.

She spun around to face him. "Don't," she quickly cut in. "It was too long ago, and it really doesn't matter," she lied. "I'm rather tired. I think I'll say good-night." Without waiting for a reply she hurried from the room.

Mitch cursed under his breath, annoyed at himself for chasing her away. He'd needed someone to listen, someone to understand the frustration he felt at the lack of progress he was making with his father.

Talking to Abby had gone a long way to help ease the burden of guilt he was still carrying, guilt that he hadn't been there when his father had needed him. Silently he marveled at how easy Abby was to talk to. She listened with a quiet understanding, offering neither judgment nor criticism, a rare quality indeed.

His thoughts shifted back to the night of his mother's death, when he'd rambled on about everything except what was really on his mind. That night he'd seen his own deep sorrow reflected in the depths of her green eyes, and felt a strong connection, a kinship he'd never been able to fully comprehend.

He'd felt it again tonight, that connection, as if they were attuned to each other on a different and higher plane, and not for the first time he wondered what there was about Abby that set her apart from other women he'd known, that touched his heart and stirred his soul.

Upstairs Abby sat at the mirrored dressing table, her thoughts drifting back over Mitch's account of the night of his mother's death. Something had puzzled her at the time but she'd let it slide.

Slowly, deliberately, she began to brush her hair, replaying the scene in the kitchen inside her head. Mitch had stated that he'd almost lost his job, that he'd been working on an assignment at the time of his mother's death, an assignment that had taken another two months to complete.

The brush fell from Abby's grasp to land with a quiet thud on the carpeted floor. *Two months.* The job had lasted another two months. The words rolled around in her head like dice in a cup, and as the implication of what it meant began to sink in, Abby felt a pain clutch at her heart.

Could that have been the reason Mitch hadn't called her? Was it possible that having already jeopardized his assignment by visiting his mother, he hadn't wanted to further break the rules by contacting her?

What *if* she'd waited? What *if* she hadn't panicked when she'd realized she was pregnant? What *if* she hadn't listened to Cal and allowed him to persuade her to accept his offer of marriage? Would things have turned out differently?

For a heart-stopping moment Abby allowed herself to believe that Mitch would have contacted her, that the assignment he'd been working on at the time was the reason he hadn't called.

But much as she might want to believe it, the fantasy quickly evaporated when she remembered that when he'd referred to their encounter, he'd said she'd taken pity on him. He believed she'd simply made love with him out of sympathy, out of a sense of pity for the loss he'd just experienced. He couldn't have been further from the truth.

The rich aroma of freshly brewed coffee greeted Abby the next morning when she came downstairs to find Mitch dressed in moss green cords and a cream-colored shirt, sitting at the kitchen table. Her pulse, as always, quickened in response and resolutely she clamped down on her errant reaction.

"You're up early," Abby commented as she crossed to the sink.

"I thought I'd go in and get some paperwork done before the store opens," he said. "By the way, tonight's the big night for Toby, isn't it?"

"If you mean the school concert, yes, it is," Abby replied after a quick glance at the calendar on the wall nearby.

"Do you think he'd mind if I tagged along?" Mitch rose and carried his cereal bowl and coffee mug to the sink.

As he approached, Abby felt her heart knock against her ribs in alarm and she quickly sidestepped out of his way to open the fridge. "No, Toby won't mind," she answered truthfully. But *she* minded; she minded very much.

She hadn't anticipated Mitch inviting himself along. She'd assumed he'd stay and keep his father company. But undoubtedly after last night's unsuccessful attempt to make peace with his father, he didn't want to spend the evening at home, and she couldn't blame him.

"Morning, Mom. Morning, Mitch," Toby greeted them as he came into the kitchen.

"Morning, Toby." They spoke in unison.

"So, are you excited about the concert tonight?" Mitch asked after he'd set the dishes in the sink.

"Yeah, I guess," Toby said, hopping up onto a chair.

"I was just telling your mom that I thought I might check it out—the concert, I mean," Mitch said.

Toby's eyes instantly lit up. "You mean you want to come with us?"

"If it's all right with you. Yes, I'd like to," Mitch said, surprised at the boy's reaction.

"Neat-o!" Toby glanced at his mother, then back at Mitch. "Want to come in our car?" Toby invited.

"How about we take my truck?" Mitch suggested. "It's better in the snow," he observed.

"Okay," Toby agreed before Abby could say anything.

"Great! Well, I'd better go," said Mitch. "See you later."

"Bye!" Toby called after his father. "You don't think he'll change his mind, do you, Mom?" Toby suddenly asked, already beginning to have doubts.

"No, I don't think so," Abby said evenly, knowing that for Toby this was a first. Cal had never shown up at any of the functions that had been put on at the preschool Toby had attended when he was four. But then, Cal had never bothered with Toby, period.

The fact that Mitch was taking an interest in Toby's school activities as well as Toby himself was a great confidence booster for the boy. And Abby knew that if Toby hadn't already developed a case of hero-worship for Mitch, this would undoubtedly have set the stage.

Abby was standing at the sink peeling potatoes while Toby sat at the kitchen table writing a letter to Santa when Mitch returned home from the store that afternoon. Toby immediately abandoned his letter writing and ran to greet his father.

"Hey, sport! All set for tonight?" Mitch asked, thinking he could easily grow accustomed to coming home each night and finding Abby and Toby waiting for him.

"Yes. Are you still coming with us?" Toby wanted to know.

"You better believe it," Mitch replied with a grin. "What time does it start?"

"Seven-thirty," Toby replied. "But I have to be there at seven, 'cause I have to get my costume on and everything," he explained.

"Then we'd better leave here about six-thirty. What do you think, Abby?" Mitch asked.

"That sounds fine," Abby replied, trying to ignore the quicksilver ripple of awareness skipping through her due solely to Mitch's presence.

"We had a dress 'hearsal after lunch today. Everybody looks neat," Toby said.

"I'm really looking forward to it," Mitch said. When he'd invited himself along he'd simply been looking for a distraction, something to take his mind off the lack of progress he was making with his father. But Toby's excitement was catching and Mitch found he was indeed looking forward to the outing. "Is that homework you're working on?" Mitch asked, noticing the sheet of paper on the kitchen table.

"No. I'm writing a letter to Santa," Toby informed him.

"Now, there's a good idea," Mitch responded. "If you get your letter off early, you'll have a better chance of getting everything on your list. What are you asking Santa for?"

"A bike," Toby announced as he returned to his seat at the table. "A two-wheeler. There's one in the window in the bike store in town. It's got gears and mag wheels, a black leather seat, a side mirror and even a headlight so you can ride it at night." Breathless, Toby came to a halt.

"Boy! That sounds like quite a bike," Mitch commented.

"Toby, darling, do me a favor, will you?" Abby said. "Run upstairs and bring down Tom's tray. I forgot to get it this afternoon."

"Okay." Toby hopped down from his chair and ran from the room.

"Is Santa bringing Toby a bike?" Mitch asked as he crossed to the table.

"It's on order," Abby replied. "I just hope it gets here before Christmas."

"How is my father today?" Mitch asked. "Did Dr. Stone pay him a visit? I passed his car heading out of town on my way to the store this morning."

"Your father's fine," Abby reported. "And yes, Dr. Stone came by about nine o'clock. He brought along a walker from the hospital."

"A walker," Mitch repeated. "And how did my father react?"

"Quite well, actually," Abby said. "Dr. Stone even managed to persuade Tom to get up and give it a try."

"Really! How did he manage that?" Mitch asked as he sat down at the table.

"Dr. Stone just told your father that if he didn't try using the walker, then he had no option but to readmit him to the hospital," Abby said.

Mitch chuckled, a warm sound that set Abby's blood humming through her veins. "Brilliant move," Mitch commented. As he spoke his gaze drifted to the letter sitting in front of him. "What happened then?" he asked.

"Tom mumbled and grumbled a bit, of course, but he finally relented," she told him. "He made it out of his bedroom, down to the end of the hall and back again. I think he even surprised himself."

"That's wonderful," Mitch said. "My bet is he's probably bored with all the inactivity." He absently scanned Toby's carefully printed letter. The bike, he noted, was indeed the first item on Toby's list. But as Mitch's gaze traveled down, he came to an abrupt halt when he read "...and I want my real Daddy."

With a puzzled frown Mitch slowly reread the phrase, thinking Toby had made an error, that he'd meant to write "...and I want a new Daddy."

"And you can drop by the hospital anytime and pick it up." Abby's voice cut into his reverie.

"What? Sorry. What's that about the hospital?" Mitch asked, frowning at the paper on the table.

Abby glanced over at Mitch. "Just that Dr. Stone said he's managed to locate a wheelchair. And you should—"

"Drop by the hospital and pick it up," Mitch finished for her. "Right, I'll do that."

"Here's the tray, Mom," Toby said as he returned to the kitchen. "Is supper ready?"

"Thanks." Abby took the tray from her son. "Supper won't be too long," she answered. "I just have to put these potatoes on to boil."

"Can I watch television for a while?" Toby asked.

"Okay," Abby said. "Oh . . . Toby, clear your stuff off the table first," she added before he could scamper away.

Toby ran to the table and quickly snatched up the letter and pencil and, with a quick grin at Mitch, dashed from the room.

By the time they were ready to leave for the concert, Toby was jumping around like a cat in a roomful of rocking chairs. Abby, who had changed into a pair of black wool slacks and a bright red mohair sweater, popped into Tom's room to say goodbye. Mitch, who had changed, too, looked stunning in a pair of gray pants and a long-sleeved charcoal shirt.

"Is there anything else you need before we go?" Abby asked as she plumped up the pillow behind Tom's head.

"Nothing, thanks. I'll be fine," Tom insisted, smiling at her. "I thought you were wearing a costume," Tom said to Toby, who had just joined them.

"I am, but it's at school," Toby said.

"Mitch was in a school concert once," Tom informed him.

"He was?" Toby glanced at Mitch, looking for confirmation.

"He's right," Mitch said. "I was a cloud."

"A cloud?" Toby repeated, breaking into a smile. "How do you dress up as a cloud?" He stifled a giggle as he stared up at Mitch.

Mitch smiled ruefully. "Well, my mother was pretty good with a sewing machine. Wasn't she, Dad?" he commented, and noted the look of pain that flashed in his father's eyes at the mention of his wife.

The air was suddenly alive with tension as father and son exchanged glances. Tempted though she was to jump in and say something to ease the strain, Abby held her breath and waited.

Tom swallowed several times before answering. "Yes, your mother was a very good seamstress," he managed to say. "If I remember correctly, she made your costume out of a white sheet and a whole lot of fluffy cotton balls."

"That's right," Mitch confirmed, pleased and encouraged by the fact that his father had actually spoken of his wife. "And you were annoyed with Mom because she used all the cotton balls you had in the store, remember?"

Tom's mouth twitched in what might have been a ghost of a smile. "Every last packet," he said. "And to top it all, thanks to those fluffy cotton balls, you spent the entire time on the stage sneezing." This time his face creased into a definite smile.

Toby started to laugh out loud, and Abby, who'd been having difficulty keeping a straight face at the image of Mitch dressed in a sheet covered with cotton balls, joined in.

For Mitch the moment was unforgettable. Hearing his father speak of his wife was a major breakthrough. But silently Mitch acknowledged that had Toby and Abby not been there, the conversation would never have taken place at all.

"I think we'd better get going," Mitch said, breaking up the fun.

"Have a good time," Tom said. "Yes, the phone's right here. And yes, I have the number of the school should I need it," he told Abby before she could ask.

All the way into town Toby talked incessantly about the concert and the songs they would be singing. The parking lot at the rear of the school was already starting to fill up as Mitch pulled the truck into an empty space.

Once inside the school building, Toby led the way to his classroom. "We'll meet you right here when it's over," Abby said. "Don't worry, you'll do just fine." She dropped a quick kiss on the top of his head.

"Good luck," Mitch said before Toby disappeared inside where the sound of excited children's voices could be heard. Turning, they made their way down the corridor to the school gymnasium.

"Mitch. Abby. Hello, there!" The greeting came from Joyce Alexander, who was walking toward them accompanied by her son Nathan, her pregnant daughter-in-law, Kit, and her grandson Mark.

After Joyce finished making introductions Abby turned to Kit. "When's the baby due?" she asked.

"Christmas Day," Kit replied with a laugh.

"Oh, how wonderful!" Abby said, a little envious of the joy and happiness she could see shining in the depths of the other woman's eyes.

"Well, I'm still trying to decide," Kit replied. "I didn't think I'd get pregnant quite this fast. But I suppose it happens that way sometimes." She threw a loving glance at her husband, who was talking to Mitch.

"Let's find some seats up front, shall we?" Joyce suggested as they reached the gymnasium. "That way we'll get a better view of Mark." She turned to Abby. "He's singing in the choir," she explained.

After Mark scooted off to join the choir Abby followed Joyce and Kit inside the beautifully decorated gymnasium. They chose seats several rows from the front and she found herself seated next to Mitch with Kit, Nathan and Joyce on the other side.

When the gymnasium was almost full, the lights dimmed and Abby, clutching her hands together in her lap, directed her attention to the stage. The moment Toby appeared dressed in his gold costume, Abby's throat closed over with emotion and she felt tears prick her eyes. As the story of the first Christmas unfolded the audience sat enthralled, smothering smiles when Joseph tripped on his costume and stifling laughter when one of the shepherds called out and waved to his parents.

She hadn't been aware of the tears trickling down her cheeks until a handkerchief was gently placed in her hands. Glancing at Mitch, she managed to smile her thanks as she accepted it and quietly blew her nose.

When the curtain slowly closed at last on the baby in the manger, Abby, along with the rest of the parents and children in attendance, loudly applauded the performance.

Moments later the curtain reopened to reveal the actors standing in the center of the stage. As the school band began to play the first bars of the hymn "Away in a Manger," everyone in the auditorium rose to their feet. Fresh tears gathered in Abby's eyes and it was all she could do to summon up her voice.

Suddenly she felt Mitch's hand gently clasp her own, sending a frisson of need chasing through her, but she had neither the willpower nor the desire to withdraw. Beside her, she heard his rich baritone voice and her heart ballooned inside her breast until she could hardly breathe.

With the aid of their conductor the young musicians and singers moved through one carol and on to another until the gymnasium rang out with the sweet and memorable sounds of Christmas.

When the last notes of "Silent Night" floated away the crowd broke into renewed applause and, glancing around, Abby noted that almost everyone seemed to be wiping moisture from their eyes.

In the scramble to unite children and parents they said their goodbyes to Joyce, Nathan and Kit, and soon everyone was making their way out to the parking lot.

"Did you like it?" Toby asked Mitch for what must have been the twentieth time.

Mitch ruffled Toby's hair before starting the truck. "*You* were terrific. All the kids were terrific," Mitch told him with a grin as he followed the line of vehicles into the street.

"I liked the part when all the animals in the stable are looking at the baby," Toby said with a tired sigh.

"I liked everything," Abby said. "Especially the three wise men." She put her arm around Toby and urged him to lean against her.

As the heater warmed the interior of the truck, Toby, exhausted from the activity and the excitement, slowly drifted off to sleep and for the remainder of the journey Abby turned her thoughts to those moments during the carol singing when Mitch had taken her hand.

Her heart skipped a beat at the memory, but she kept her gaze focused on the road ahead, all the while thinking this would be a night she would never forget. Outside, the snow looked eerily bright and as she gazed up at the stars twinkling like Christmas lights in the blue-black sky, she closed her eyes and made a wish.

"Abby, we're home." Mitch's softly spoken words brought her instantly awake.

"Sorry, I must have dozed off," Abby murmured, noting that Mitch was already reaching for the driver's door.

"Toby, darling," Abby said, gently nudging him awake.

"Here, slide over this way, Toby, and I'll carry you inside," Mitch suggested.

"Okay," Toby murmured sleepily as he followed Mitch's instructions and slid across the seat.

Abby quickly climbed from the truck to open the front door. Mitch, with a sleepy-eyed boy in his arms, crossed to the stairs. "There you go, sport," Mitch said as he lowered Toby onto the bottom step. Toby yawned in response.

"Think you can make it upstairs on your own?" Mitch asked, still crouched in front of the boy.

Toby nodded and managed a smile.

"You did a great job tonight, Toby," Mitch said. "Your father would have been proud of you."

The smile vanished from Toby's face and he began to shake his head. "No, he wouldn't," Toby replied, wide awake now.

Surprised at the boy's reaction, Mitch frowned and, still crouching, put his hand on Toby's shoulder. "I think your father would have been very proud of you," Mitch repeated.

"No, he wouldn't!" Toby's voice was much louder this time, anger evident in his tone. "He wouldn't have been proud 'cause he wasn't my father. He told me so!" he added almost defiantly. And with that Toby turned and raced up the stairs.

Chapter Seven

Mitch rose from his crouched position and stared in stunned surprise at Toby's departing figure. He turned to Abby in time to see an expression of shock and dismay on her face. As his gaze met hers, an emotion he instantly recognized as guilt flashed in her eyes.

"Abby? What...?" Bewildered, Mitch frantically tried to make sense of Toby's comment. If what the boy said was true... If Cal wasn't Toby's father, then who...

As Mitch tried to wrestle with the implications, he realized that Abby had crossed to where he stood at the bottom of the stairs, her intention obviously to go after the boy.

"Hold on a minute," he said, anger edging into his tone now as he blocked her way. "Toby isn't lying, is he? Cal wasn't his father. But if that's true, then who—" He stopped, seeing the flicker of fear that danced in her eyes.

"Toby needs me," she said huskily, attempting to move past him. But Mitch held his ground. All at once Abby's conversation with Kit earlier at the school jumped into his mind. Kit had said something about being surprised at how fast she'd become pregnant, but adding that it happened sometimes.

Mitch cast his mind back seven years, probing his memory, searching for some confirmation of what he was thinking. He knew Toby was six years old, but he didn't know the exact date of Toby's birth, and while Mitch had at the time fleetingly considered the possibility of Abby becoming pregnant the night he'd made love with her, he'd dismissed the notion when he'd learned she was marrying Cal Roberts.

But what other reason could there be for the fear he'd seen in her eyes on the day he'd arrived home, or for that matter some of the behavior she'd demonstrated since?

"I think I'm entitled to the truth," Mitch said, his tone ominous.

Abby, her head bent, swallowed convulsively, determined to keep her emotions in check. The disaster she'd been anticipating from the moment Mitch had appeared on the doorstep had come to pass. But right now the most important person to consider was Toby. "Please, can this wait? Toby needs me," she repeated, a plea for understanding in her voice.

"All right." Mitch relented. "I'll be in the kitchen. We need to talk."

Abby nodded and Mitch instantly stepped aside. Upstairs she found Toby lying on his bed, crying, his face buried in his pillow. "It's all right, Toby. Don't cry, darling," Abby said as she sat beside him and pulled his unresisting body into her arms.

That Cal had told Toby he wasn't his father had come as a shock to Abby. Cal had paid little attention to the boy, rarely bothering to speak to him. Anger flared to life within her that Cal could have been so cruel.

"He wasn't my real dad, was he?" Toby asked as he eased away to look at her, his eyes searching her face as if he was looking for confirmation.

Pain and guilt tugged at her heart. Toby deserved the truth. "No, he wasn't your real father," Abby replied, and watched as a look of relief settled over Toby's tearstained face. "I'm sorry he hurt you, Toby," Abby said, fighting back tears.

"Don't cry, Mom," Toby said. "It's all right. Really it s." He hugged her tightly once more.

Abby clung to her son, silently berating herself for not aving had the courage to leave Cal, for staying on in a narriage that hadn't been a marriage at all.

But, on reflection, she knew hadn't had much choice in he matter. She'd used her savings to put herself through the ursing program at the university, and once she'd gradu-ted, the money she'd earned as a nurse had gone to pay ent and other living expenses.

After her marriage to Cal, she'd moved in to his two-edroom apartment and at his gentle insistence had agreed o let him take care of their finances. Cal had assured her he didn't have to work, and at first Abby had been touched y this show of consideration, until she realized that with-ut a job she had no money of her own, no means of sup-orting herself.

That's when Cal's true colors had started to emerge. By ontrolling their financial situation he also controlled her, nd he'd made sure that she had no access to any bank ac-ounts. Whenever she'd needed money she'd had to ask for t and tell him exactly what the money was being used for. Ie'd enjoyed the power he had over her and she was rapped like a prisoner, dependent on him for everything.

Abby stroked Toby's hair and murmured words of com-ort until at last, exhausted, he fell asleep. After undress-ng him and tucking him into bed she lingered upstairs as ong as she dared, even peeking in on Tom in the hope that e might be awake and delay her confrontation with Mitch. But there was to be no respite. Tom was asleep.

Bracing herself for what was to come, she slowly made er way downstairs. As she entered the kitchen her pulse icked up speed at the sight of Mitch standing with his back o her, staring out into the night.

"I was just thinking about coming to get you," Mitch aid as he turned to face her. "I poured myself a brandy. Vould you like one?" His tone was polite, but Abby could eel the tension in the air and sensed, too, the effort it was aking for Mitch to keep his anger in check.

"No, thank you," Abby managed to say.

Mitch met her gaze, his eyes glittering like sapphires, and she felt her heart trip over itself in reaction. "Is Toby my son?" he asked, cutting directly to the crux of the matter.

Abby's mouth suddenly felt like a piece of sandpaper and she couldn't for the life of her make her vocal cords respond. And so she nodded. She watched as a look of joy flared in his eyes, before it was replaced by another emotion less easy to define. Her knees began to tremble and, like an aftershock from an earthquake, her whole body also began to shake.

"Are you sure?" Mitch asked, his voice as cold as the winter wind outside. "There was a rumor circulating—" He broke off when he saw surprise then pain flash in the depths of her green eyes.

"Toby is your son." Abby forced the words out, shocked beyond belief by what Mitch had just implied; that someone other than him had fathered her child. It didn't take her long to reach the obvious conclusion that Cal had undoubtedly been the source of whatever rumor Mitch had mentioned. Fresh anger at the lengths Cal had gone to control and isolate her coursed through Abby, effectively stilling her trembling body.

"Why didn't you contact me?" Mitch demanded "Damn it, Abby, I had a right to know. And if you were pregnant with my child, why the hell did you marry Roberts?" Mitch came to a halt, but she could see the suppressed fury in every line of his body.

But Abby refused to accept all the blame. "Contact you! And just how was I supposed to do that when you vanished like a thief in the night without as much as a good bye?" she countered. "I waited for you to call me, and when you didn't..." She ground to a halt, her voice wavering, fighting back the tears suddenly threatening to overwhelm her.

"I couldn't call," Mitch replied. "I was on an assignment, an assignment I'd already jeopardized by going to visit my mother in the hospital."

"How was I supposed to know that?" Abby challenged "Maybe if you'd told me. Maybe if you'd left a note—" She broke off. They were getting nowhere and there wa little point in simply exchanging accusations. Bravely she met his gaze. "When I realized I was pregnant, I panicked—"

"And ran to Cal," Mitch finished for her. "Of course, why not? You were dating him."

Abby drew a steadying breath. "Yes, I'd dated Cal, but—"

"Then how can you be so sure Toby isn't his son?" The air between them sizzled with renewed tension. Mitch's automatic assumption that she'd slept with Cal was like a blow to Abby's heart, and while she understood Mitch's anger and his need to lash out at her, she felt as if he'd tried and convicted her without bothering to ascertain if she was guilty of the crime.

"Because I hadn't slept with Cal, that's why," Abby said, managing with difficulty to maintain control, refraining from telling Mitch that on the night he'd made love to her she'd been a virgin, foolishly giving her body to the man she thought would honor both her and the gift she had given. But instead he'd simply taken what she offered and walked away without a second thought.

"Did Cal know I was the baby's father?" Mitch wanted to know.

"Yes," Abby confirmed, feeling it was pointless to lie. She'd planned to keep Mitch's identity a secret, but Cal had coaxed her into telling him the truth and she remembered now the flash of anger she'd seen in his eyes at her disclosure.

"You told Roberts, but you didn't bother to contact me?" Mitch challenged angrily.

Abby bristled at his tone. "I don't remember waking up and finding your telephone number pinned to my pillow," she quickly countered, annoyed that he seemed intent on throwing the blame at her feet. "This is getting us nowhere," she added with a tired sigh. Hadn't he been the one who'd told her he'd believed she'd taken pity on him that night?

"Why did you marry him?" Mitch asked again, unsure why he was pursuing the question, but unable to under-

stand what had prompted Abby to accept a man like Cal as
her husband.

"I was pregnant and alone, with nowhere to turn. Cal
was there," she told him, wondering, not for the first time,
why she hadn't talked to one of the counselors at the hospital. But then, she hadn't really been thinking straight and
Cal had seemed genuinely concerned, anxious to help.

When she'd asked Cal if he knew Mitch, he'd told her
Mitch worked in a different department, that he didn't
know him very well. He'd offered to talk to Mitch for her,
but Abby had rejected the idea, having already reached the
conclusion that their passionate encounter had meant
nothing to him.

Cal had been lying to her then as he'd lied all along, but
she'd been too distressed and emotionally overwrought to
see that he was manipulating her. His offer of marriage had
come a short time later and, while she'd been moved by his
concern for her welfare, she'd turned him down, at least at
first. But he'd urged her to reconsider, pointing out that it
was a viable solution to the dilemma she faced, adding that
if she wasn't able to financially support herself and her
child, the child might easily be taken from her.

It wasn't true, of course. But he'd succeeded in fright-
ening her. And so she'd accepted Cal's proposal, naively
believing she knew what she was getting into even when he
told her their marriage would be real in every way.

But Cal had been an impatient and inconsiderate lover
taking his own pleasure and leaving her feeling used and
degraded. As her pregnancy had advanced, his interest in
her had diminished, and it wasn't until after Toby's birth
that she'd begun to notice the telltale signs, signs Cal hadn'
bothered to hide, signs that he was seeing another woman

When she'd confronted him, he'd readily confirmed her
suspicions and, thinking this was her chance to break free
of a marriage she should never have agreed to, she'd asked
for a divorce. He'd adamantly refused, stating she was his
wife and that nothing would ever change that.

In an act of defiance she'd moved her things into Toby'
room and had been relieved when Cal hadn't protested or
forced himself on her.

Agreeing to marry Cal had been the worst decision of her life, but no matter how much she might want to blame Cal, she had allowed herself to be his victim.

"Damn it, Abby. You should have told me." Mumbling under his breath, Mitch spun away and reached for the brandy glass on the table. Tossing the remainder of the contents into his mouth, he savored the bite and the heat of the liquid as it trickled down his throat.

He was still desperately trying to come to terms with the knowledge that he had a son. But while he'd had a gut feeling Abby hadn't been lying when she told him Toby was his, he'd had to ask, had to push her to the wall, had to be sure.

A son! He had a son! Toby was his own flesh and blood, and at this thought a feeling of joy engulfed him once more and it was all he could do not to yell out in jubilation.

"Why didn't you come and tell me about Toby after Cal died?" His question brought him back to face her. "Why didn't you tell me then?" he asked, and watched as Abby moistened her lips with her tongue, an action that had his stomach muscles tightening in response.

"Would you have believed me?" she asked, her voice low. Meeting his gaze, she saw the hesitation, the flash of indecision in the depths of his eyes. "I didn't think so," she went on. "That's why I didn't tell you. That's why I did what I thought was best for Toby."

Mitch had no reply. Silently he acknowledged that she was probably right. He wouldn't have believed her if she'd come to him after Cal's death.

"What are you going to do?" Abby's question cut through his musings and he refocused his attention on the woman before him, noting the fear and anxiety in the depths of her green eyes.

"I don't know. I just don't know," he repeated, dragging a hand through his hair in a gesture of frustration and uncertainty.

Abby bit back the sob threatening to break free. "I'm rather tired," she said thickly. "I'm going to bed." She turned and made her way from the room.

Mitch made no protest. While his initial anger had dissipated, he found his thoughts and emotions in complete upheaval. He needed to think, to get in touch with his feelings, to explore and analyze his options.

Throughout his career he'd often had to make split-second decisions, and he'd come to rely on his instincts, on his gut feelings. But this was different. This decision could well be one of the most important of his life.

Pulling out a kitchen chair, Mitch sat down and, leaning on his elbows, rested his head on his hands. Closing his eyes, he cast his mind back, as he had done so many times during the past seven years, to the night he and Abby had made love.

When she'd found him that night wandering through the hospital corridors, he'd been emotionally distraught and somewhat disoriented. At first he hadn't recognized the beautiful young woman in the nurse's uniform as being the same shy cashier he'd made friends with that summer he'd spent in Peachville, prior to joining the police force.

Not wanting to be alone, he'd accepted her offer of a cup of coffee and, once in her tiny apartment, had found her easy to talk to. He'd asked her questions about her life, steering clear of the subject of his mother, wanting to keep the feeling of emptiness in his heart at bay. Abby had taken her cue from him and chatted about anything and everything except his mother's death.

When he'd risen to leave he'd seen the look of understanding and compassion in her eyes, and he'd been moved immeasurably when she'd reached up to touch his cheek in a show of silent sympathy. His throat had instantly closed over with emotion and he'd bent to kiss her, purely in a gesture of thanks.

But the moment his mouth had touched hers, he'd suddenly understood the meaning of "spontaneous combustion." Never before had he experienced such heat, such need, such passion. Like a forest fire raging out of control, the flames had quickly engulfed them, igniting a desire they could neither ignore nor control.

He'd awakened just before dawn and gazed in awe at the woman beside him as an emotion he hadn't recognized tugged at his heart. Tempted though he'd been to taste again the nectar of her lips and rekindle the passion they'd shared, he'd clamped down on the need humming through his veins. Slipping silently out of bed, he'd tiptoed from the room.

Anticipating the panic his disappearance had undoubtedly caused, he'd felt that his first priority was to return to his post and reestablish his contacts. It had crossed his mind to leave Abby a note, but he'd felt reasonably sure that if the undercover operation hadn't already been blown, it would wind up in a few days and he would contact her then.

He couldn't have been more wrong.

He'd let himself out and after waving down a cruising cab had returned to the underworld, but instead of the assignment reaching a quick conclusion it had dragged on for another two months.

Yes, he had to shoulder at least part of the blame, Mitch thought with a sigh. He'd been too wrapped up in his own world, too concerned about other things, to take the time to consider how Abby would feel when she woke and found him gone.

But what about Roberts? Had Cal played a part in depriving him of the knowledge he'd fathered a child? Roberts had married Abby knowing she was carrying another man's child, his child. Somehow Mitch couldn't quite picture Cal in the role of white knight. Not unless there was something in it for Cal.

Pushing himself away from the table, Mitch rose and began to pace. There had never been any love lost between himself and Roberts, not since those early days of basic training when Mitch had outshone him in every aspect.

Could Roberts have borne him a grudge all these years? Could Cal have used Abby's predicament as a means of extracting revenge? Drastic though that seemed, Mitch couldn't quite shake the notion that he just might be right.

Mitch recalled with a frown the day Roberts had announced his upcoming marriage to Abby. His appearance in the detectives' squad room that morning had been uncommon to say the least, and on reflection Mitch realized that there had been a smugness about the man, a self-satisfied look Mitch hadn't fully comprehended at the time.

He was probably barking up the wrong tree. Maybe Roberts had come to Abby's aid out of the goodness of his heart and he was simply clutching at straws, looking to throw some blame Roberts's way.

But the news of Abby's pending marriage to Cal had left a bitter taste in Mitch's mouth, and he knew without a doubt that had she been marrying anyone else he would have gone to see her, to find out if she was truly happy with her decision. But he hadn't, and he regretted that now...in fact, he regretted a number of things.

Silently Mitch acknowledged he was unlikely to ever learn the whole truth. What was more important was the present and the future. Toby, the boy he'd come to love like a son, was indeed his son and, regardless of blame, that fact would never change.

But even as he savored this knowledge, even as it filled him with a new warmth and a sense of wonder, he was no nearer making a decision about the future than he'd been on the day he arrived.

Abby spent a restless night wondering and worrying what Mitch would do now that he knew the truth about Toby. As she stood in the shower the next morning she thought again about their conversation in the kitchen. She remembered clearly the look of joy she'd seen in his eyes when she'd told him Toby was his son, and not for the first time Abby wondered what would have happened if she hadn't panicked and turned to Cal.

While part of her wanted to believe Mitch would have done the right thing seven years ago and asked her to marry him, another part, a more pragmatic part, quietly faced the reality that statistics showed a marriage entered into under those conditions often had little chance of survival.

The fact that she'd believed herself to be madly in love with Mitch when he'd made love with her that night had little bearing on the matter. Ever since the age of sixteen she'd dreamed and fantasized about Mitch and what it would feel to have him kiss her, touch her, make love with her. When the fantasy had suddenly become a reality, she hadn't had the willpower to deny herself what she'd been secretly dreaming about for years.

But she'd grown up a lot since then—she'd had to—and ever since Cal's death, ever since she'd regained her freedom and independence, she'd shied away from men and relationships. She was determined she and Toby would make it on their own, vowing never to let herself become involved with any man who looked on her as his property.

Turning off the water, Abby stepped from the shower and wrapped herself in a towel. While she doubted Mitch had any legal recourse with regard to Toby, she had no intention of depriving him of a chance to get to know his son, if that's what he wanted.

And what about Toby? Now that she'd confirmed that Cal wasn't his father, it was only a matter of time until Toby started asking questions about his real father. He deserved to know the truth, if only to help erase some of the pain caused by Cal's cruel and callous treatment.

That Toby would be thrilled to learn Mitch was his father was an understatement, but by telling him the truth now, Abby wondered if she would simply be setting him up for more disappointment. Because when the holiday season was over and Mitch returned to his job in Vancouver, Abby had a feeling Toby wouldn't be the only one who'd miss him when he left.

Abby dressed in navy stirrup pants and a pastel green sweater and with practiced ease braided her shoulder-length hair. Downstairs, the empty cereal bowl and coffee cup in the sink told her Mitch had already breakfasted. Taking a look outside, she noted with some relief that his truck no longer stood in the driveway.

"How was the concert?" Tom asked when Abby brought him his breakfast tray a short time later.

"Wonderful," Abby replied with a smile, recalling with a pang those unforgettable moments when Mitch had held her hand. "Toby played his part beautifully," she reported proudly.

"He's a great kid," Tom said. "Reminds me of Mitch when he was that age," he added, and Abby had to fight off the impulse to tell Tom just why that was so.

"Mmm," she said as she crossed to the hospital walker Dr. Stone had brought in the previous day. "Do you feel like taking a jaunt down the hall again today?" she asked.

Tom glanced up from his plate of eggs on toast. "Oh, I suppose I could give it another go," he said nonchalantly.

"Good," Abby said, trying not to smile. Tom was tiring of his role of invalid, and while Abby was pleased he was taking an interest in getting mobile, she reminded herself that once Tom was back on his feet and able to take care of himself she would be out of a job.

"Has Mitch left yet?" Tom asked.

"Yes, as a matter of fact he has," Abby said. "Is there something you wanted?"

"No...no. At least, it's not urgent or anything...." Tom trailed off. "It's Sunday tomorrow, the store's closed. He could do it then," he added.

"Do what?" Abby asked, frowning in puzzlement.

"Well, I've been thinking. It's been a long time since there's been a child in the house...and well, what with Christmas just around the corner—I thought Mitch could drive you and Toby over to the Simpson farm to pick out a Christmas tree."

Abby felt tears prick her eyes. "Tom, that's a lovely idea," she said and watched as his face turned bright pink. "I'm sure Toby would love to pick out a tree," she added, deciding that she would excuse herself from the outing.

"I haven't put up a Christmas tree in years," Tom went on, and Abby's heart ached at the pain and loneliness she could hear in his voice. "The decorations are in the attic. Mitch can bring them down." He smiled weakly. "By the way, where is Toby this morning? I haven't heard him running around."

"He's still asleep. Too much excitement last night," she told him. "Enjoy your breakfast. I'll be back to get your tray in a little while." She crossed to the door. "We can give the walker a try then, if you like," she added over her shoulder before heading to Toby's room.

Toby was indeed still asleep and Abby quietly withdrew. Generally Toby rose early on Saturday mornings, but after the trauma of the night before she wasn't surprised he was sleeping late.

She hoped when he awoke that last night's incident would have faded somewhat from his mind. Toby's memories of Cal had diminished, but while his reaction last night had been understandable it had also been upsetting.

In the kitchen Abby sipped on her coffee and gazed outside at the beautiful winter scene. Since the storm earlier in the week had passed through, the landscape had changed very little. The temperature had remained constant at a few degrees below zero and the snow showed no signs of melting. Abby watched as a robin flew from branch to snowy branch in search of food, stopping momentarily to sing a few sweet notes.

"Mom?"

Abby turned to see Toby in his pajamas. "Hello, sweetheart," Abby said with a smile. "Are you hungry?"

Toby nodded and crossed to take his seat at the table. "Has Mitch gone?" Toby asked, his expression anxious.

Abby's heart skipped a beat. "He's gone to work at the store," she told him as she removed a cereal bowl from the cupboard.

"Is he mad at me?" Toby asked, worry evident in his eyes.

"No, darling, Mitch isn't mad at you," Abby assured him and saw her son's features relax a little. "How about a bowl of oatmeal?" she asked, hoping to redirect his thoughts away from the events of the previous night.

"Okay," Toby replied, his tone still subdued. "Mom?"

"Yes, Toby?" Abby responded evenly, sensing that Toby was about to ask an important question.

"What happened to my real dad?"

Abby's hands stilled for a moment and she drew a steadying breath, wondering how best to answer, grateful for the fact that Mitch had already gone, though she doubted Toby would have approached the subject had Mitch been there.

"Nothing happened to him," Abby said after a lengthy pause. "Things just didn't work out between your father

and me, that's all." She knew she was being deliberately
vague but wanted to wait until Mitch gave her some indication of how he intended to deal with the situation.

"Why not?" Toby wanted to know.

Abby crossed to the table and sat down next to her son.
"Your father didn't love me," she said, and felt a fresh
wave of pain wash over her. She swallowed convulsively.
"When I realized I was going to have a baby...when I
found out I was going to have you, I was so happy." She
reached out to gently touch his cheek. "But I didn't know
how I was going to take care of you on my own, and I got
frightened," she told him truthfully. "Cal offered to help.
And when he asked me to marry him, I thought it would be
all right, I thought he would love us and take care of us. But
I was wrong. I'm sorry, Toby. Sorry that he hurt you—"
She broke off as tears threatened once more.

"I didn't mean to make you cry, Mom," Toby said, his
expression anxious.

Abby shook her head and wiped away a stray tear. "I'm
all right," she reassured him, summoning up a smile. "And
we've been managing fine on our own, just the two of us.
Haven't we?" she asked, needing some reassurance herself.

Toby nodded but Abby could see the wistful look in her
son's eyes, telling her clearly how much he longed for a father.

"I thought I'd bake Christmas cookies this morning,"
Abby said, brightly changing the topic. "Want to give me
a hand?"

"Okay," said Toby.

"I'd better give you your breakfast," she said, rising
from the chair. Crossing to the counter, Abby quickly
mixed hot water in the bowl of dry cereal.

"Can I eat it in front of the television?" Toby asked
hopefully.

"Sure," Abby replied, and was rewarded with a smile
from her son. "Here, I'll carry it in for you," she added as
she gathered up the bowl and place mat.

Abby left Toby in front of the television and headed upstairs. To her surprise Tom was seated on the edge of the

bed in his dressing gown. With Abby looking on, Tom made the journey from his bedroom to the end of the hall several times, and with each trip his confidence increased and his smile grew wider.

Toby appeared to cheer Tom's efforts, and once he was settled back in bed, Abby delivered a fresh cup of coffee to his room.

For the remainder of the day Abby kept both herself and Toby busy making Christmas cookies. But as the afternoon wore on and she began to prepare the evening meal, her glance strayed to the clock on the wall in anticipation of Mitch's return.

As for Toby, every time he heard the sound of a car or truck go by on the road he would rush into the living room to see if Mitch had returned. At six-thirty, more than an hour past Mitch's usual time, Abby stood at the stove stirring the pot of spaghetti sauce, trying with difficulty to stop her imagination from supplying vivid pictures of Mitch's body sprawled in the front seat of his truck or lying bleeding somewhere on the road.

When she heard Toby's yelp of excitement followed by the deep tones of Mitch's voice she almost sagged with relief, quickly bracing herself for his appearance. It was hard to believe that after only a week his presence had come to mean so much to both her and Toby. Tom, too, had undergone a change since Mitch's return, and Abby felt confident that a reconciliation between the two men wasn't as far away as Mitch seemed to think.

"Sorry I'm late," Mitch said when he entered the kitchen. "The delivery truck broke down this afternoon, so I stopped to make a few deliveries on the way home."

"No problem," Abby assured him, warmed by his apology as well as the explanation for his tardiness. Glancing at Mitch, she felt her heart jolt against her rib cage in a reaction that was becoming all too familiar.

"Mr. Tom walked up and down the hall upstairs today," Toby told Mitch.

"Did he? That's good to hear," Mitch said. "And what did you do today, Toby?" he asked. Crossing to the sink, he proceeded to wash his hands.

"Mom and I baked cookies, and I finished my letter to Santa. Then I played checkers with Mr. Tom. I won two times and he won once," Toby said in a rush as he climbed up onto his chair.

Abby slowly lowered the spaghetti noodles into the pot of boiling water on the back burner of the stove.

"Sounds like you had a fun day," Mitch commented as he dried his hands on the towel nearby. "Hmm...that spaghetti sauce smells good." He came up behind Abby and leaned toward her to gaze down at the sauce simmering on the stove.

Abby's breath caught in her throat as his body brushed briefly against hers, and it was all she could do not to turn into his arms, so strong was the need suddenly clutching at her insides.

"Oh...excuse me. I forgot to check the garlic bread," she mumbled as she moved to the oven.

Mitch threw Abby a puzzled glance as she scurried away. Though he'd been busy at the store for most of the day, he'd found his thoughts continually turning to Toby, his son, and instantly a warmth would steal over him together with a feeling of wonder.

Throughout the night he'd tossed and turned as his mind played the *What if* game. *What if* he had awakened Abby that morning seven years ago and given her a brief explanation of why she might not hear from him for a while? *What if* she had contacted him and told him she was pregnant? *What if* he'd gone to see Abby before he headed into the office that day, the day Roberts had made his startling announcement about his pending marriage to Abby? *What if? What if?* The possibilities had been endless, but the fact remained that none of those scenarios had taken place.

And even if they had, Mitch wasn't altogether sure what the outcome would have been, or how he would have reacted to the news that he was to become a father. While his head was telling him that he would have done the right thing, that he would have asked Abby to marry him, the question remained. Would she have accepted?

During his conversation with Abby the previous night, when he'd tried to determine the reason she'd married

Roberts, she'd seemed reluctant to talk about him, simply stating that Cal had been both supportive and sensitive to the predicament she'd found herself in.

That Abby had married Roberts at all still rankled more than he was willing to admit, and Mitch wasn't altogether sure what to think about that. What angered him more was the fact that Cal had obviously cared very little for the child. Why else would he have told Toby he wasn't his real father? Such an announcement was not only insensitive but inordinately cruel.

But much as he might resent Roberts and question his motives, he'd been there for Abby at a time when she'd needed support, and Mitch had to accept that Abby had obviously cared about Cal and cared deeply. Why else would she have agreed to marry him?

Chapter Eight

"Would you like to take up your father's tray?"

Abby's question cut through Mitch's wayward thoughts, but before he could reply the telephone rang. "I'll get it," he offered, noting Abby had her hands full. "Hello! Kit! How are you?"

Abby grated fresh Parmesan cheese on top of Tom's plate of spaghetti wondering, when she heard Mitch's greeting, if Kit had called to talk to her. But after a quick glance at Mitch she saw he was listening attentively.

Unsure just how long he would be on the telephone, Abby picked up Tom's tray and headed upstairs. When she returned a few minutes later it was to hear Mitch sign off.

"Thanks again, Kit. See you next Friday night. Bye," he said.

"Who's Kit? And why are you seeing her on Friday?" Toby asked when Mitch replaced the receiver.

"Toby, don't be rude," Abby scolded as she carried the bowl of spaghetti to the table.

"Kit is a lady your mother and I met at the school concert last night," Mitch said. "She's Mark Alexander's mother. Do you know Mark?"

"Yeah. He goes to my school," Toby said, and handed his plate to his mother.

"That's right," Mitch replied. Picking up the basket of garlic bread from the counter, he set it on the table. "Kit and her husband, Nathan, are having a dinner party next Friday evening. She called to invite your mother and me."

Abby's head jerked up in surprise.

"Can I come, too?" Toby wanted to know.

"Sorry, sport." Mitch softened his rebuff with a smile. "It's for grown-ups. You'd probably be bored, anyway, because we'll just be sitting around talking," he explained as he sat down.

"It's very nice of Kit to invite me," Abby said, warmed by the fact that she had been included in the invitation. "But I don't think I should accept," she added.

Mitch threw her a puzzled glance. "Why not?" he asked.

"Well...I..." She faltered, taken aback by his question. "I can't leave Toby on his own," she finished lamely, careful to avoid Mitch's gaze as she scooped pasta onto her son's plate.

"But he won't be on his own," Mitch said. "My father's here, remember?"

Abby concentrated on preventing the noodles from sliding onto the table. "Yes, I know," she said. "But I can't expect your father to baby-sit—"

"I'm not a baby, Mom," Toby declared, sounding more than a little piqued by his mother's reference.

"I know you're not darling, but—" Abby tried to continue, feeling as if she was being bombarded from both sides.

"You should go, Mom," Toby cut in. "Me and Mr. Tom will be fine. You never go to parties or to a movie or anywhere," Toby continued, warming up to the topic. "Molly's mom goes out all the time. Molly is my friend at school," he told Mitch. "Molly says her mom is always going on dates. Is going to a party like a date?" Toby wanted to know.

Mitch managed to keep his smile in check. "I suppose you could say it's a date," he responded. Casting a quick glance at Abby, he was in time to see an emotion flicker briefly in the depths of her green eyes, an emotion he couldn't quite decipher.

"No, really…it doesn't matter." Abby felt her face grow warm and tried with difficulty to slow her racing heart. It was bad enough that Toby had intervened at all, but she wished he hadn't referred to the outing as a date. She'd never been on a date with Mitch and the idea sent a shiver of longing down her spine.

"Don't you want to go on a date with Mitch?" Toby asked innocently.

Abby's hands stilled at the question and she had to swallow the lump of emotion suddenly clogging her throat. The silence was somehow intimidating as both Mitch and Toby waited for her response.

"It's not that…" she began tentatively.

"So you'll go?" Toby said, interpreting her reply as a yes.

"Well…I—I—" She stammered to a halt. Two pairs of pale blue eyes stared at her and Abby felt like a deer trapped in the headlights of a car. "All right. I'll go," she said, acknowledging defeat, knowing that to argue further would only result in more questions. Besides, she liked the Alexander family and the outing would be a pleasant change. And it wasn't as if it was a real date.

Later as she lay in bed staring at the ceiling, Abby began to have second thoughts about accepting Kit's invitation. Since Cal's death two years ago she'd struggled to make ends meet and make a life for herself and Toby. Most of the money she'd earned had gone to pay for rent and groceries as well as clothes for her growing son.

The only item in her meager wardrobe that might prove suitable for the dinner party was a black dress she'd bought four years ago to wear to a New Year's party she and Cal had been invited to.

Mrs. Jones, their next-door neighbor in the apartment building, had offered to baby-sit for them, and Abby had been looking forward to the party for several weeks. She'd been dressed and ready to go when Cal came off duty that night, but within minutes he'd told her he'd changed his mind, that he'd volunteered to work an extra shift. Abby remembered how disappointed she'd been at the time, but she'd known that an argument with Cal was an exercise in futility.

She'd kept the dress, hoping one day to wear it, but recalling its scooped neckline both back and front she wasn't altogether sure the style would be appropriate. Added to that, of course, was the nerve-racking fact that she'd be spending the evening with Mitch in what might in ordinary circumstances be regarded as a date.

This thought sent a fresh ripple of awareness chasing through her, and not for the first time she wondered what there was about Mitch that affected her so profoundly. But she'd never been able to forget him or the way he'd made her feel that night so long ago. With one kiss he'd unlocked the door to her sensuality, awakened her body to the delights and ultimate heights of passion with a tenderness and sensitivity that had touched her soul.

Sunday morning dawned and Abby awakened with a start, surprised to discover that she'd overslept. Scrambling out of bed, she dressed and hurried downstairs, to be met with the appetizing aroma of bacon cooking.

"Good morning," Mitch greeted her cheerfully as she entered the kitchen.

"Good morning," she acknowledged. "Ah... I overslept. I'm sorry. Your father, has he...?" Abby began, feeling like a schoolgirl offering her teacher an excuse for being late for class.

"No problem," Mitch said. "I already took him up his breakfast. Have a seat," he added. "Do you like bacon and eggs?" He threw the question over his shoulder.

"Yes, but—" Abby said, feeling a little bewildered.

"One egg or two?" he interrupted.

"One," she answered automatically. "But you don't have to—"

"And toast?" he continued, overriding her protests.

"Ah, yes... thank you," Abby responded, a warmth stealing over her at Mitch's gentle bullying. It had been a long time since anyone had made breakfast for her, or done anything for her, for that matter. She was accustomed to looking after herself, and Toby of course, and she couldn't remember the last time someone had pampered her or treated her with such consideration. "Is Toby still in bed?" she asked, suddenly wondering why he hadn't come into her room to wake her as he usually did on a Sunday morning.

"No, he's watching TV," Mitch replied. "He wanted to wake you, but I told him to let you sleep," he explained. "Sit down. It's almost ready."

Abby crossed to the table and sat down. Within minutes Mitch set a plate before her with six pieces of crispy bacon, an egg cooked just the way she liked it, and two slices of whole wheat toast.

"Thank you," Abby said, touched by his gesture.

"Breakfast is my specialty," he told her with a grin that sent her pulse skyrocketing. "By the way," he continued, "my father suggested I take you and Toby over to the Simpson farm to pick out a Christmas tree this morning."

"Oh, yes, Tom mentioned something about that yesterday," Abby said, wishing Mitch would move away, sure that he could see her pulse fluttering at her throat, entirely due to the fact that he was standing much too close. "I know Toby would love to go," she managed to say before biting into a piece of bacon.

"Aren't you coming with us?" Mitch asked.

Abby shook her head. "Thanks, but I'll stay here with your father and get him to try the walker again," she answered. "He needs to do a little every day."

"Fine," Mitch said, hiding his disappointment. When his father had suggested he take Abby and Toby to pick out a tree, Mitch had remembered with great fondness those trips he, his mother and father had made to the Simpson farm each Christmas.

While it was somehow fitting that he take Toby with him this year to reestablish the old family tradition, he wished Abby was going with them. That she was trying to give him time alone with his son was undoubtedly the reason for her refusal, but as far as Mitch was concerned choosing a tree had always been a family outing.

Mitch and Toby left for the Simpson farm a short time later, and after clearing away her breakfast dishes Abby made her way upstairs to Tom's room. To her surprise she found him dressed in his housecoat and sitting on the edge of his bed.

"All ready to give it a try, I see," she said with a smile.

"I'm getting kinda tired of staring at these four walls," Tom admitted ruefully.

Tom was indeed making progress and soon made several trips down the hall and back. "You're doing really well," Abby commented as she watched him turn around in the hallway. "If you keep this up, you won't be needing me for too much longer." She kept her tone light, hiding the twinge of anxiety she felt at the prospect of having to find another job.

Tom shook his head. "I'm not ready to be left to my own devices just yet," he told her. "Besides, I rather like having you and Toby around to keep me company. I doubt Mitch will hang around here any longer than he feels necessary. His job always comes first. That's dedication for you." He sighed. "I sure wish he'd married some nice girl and supplied me with a few grandchildren. But he married that job of his instead."

Abby heard the longing in Tom's voice and her heart went out to him. Tempted as she was to tell him about Toby, she kept silent, deciding to wait until Mitch voiced his intentions regarding the boy.

When she'd accepted the job as Tom's nurse and housekeeper she'd seen it as a means for Tom and his grandfather to get to know each other. That a friendship had formed between them had been an added bonus, and Abby silently hoped that Mitch wouldn't be opposed to his father knowing the truth.

"This is getting too easy," Tom said as he made the turn into his bedroom. "I'll have to try the stairs next time."

Encouraged as she was by his progress, Abby knew that stairs were a more difficult proposition. "Maybe we should wait a few days on that," she suggested as she followed him into his room.

"Phew...maybe you're right," Tom acknowledged. "I'm worn out. I'm about ready for a nap."

"Good idea. I'll leave you to it," Abby said after she'd seen him safely into bed.

Returning to the kitchen, Abby proceeded to make a pot of vegetable soup. As she chopped and diced the vegetables, she wondered just what she and Toby would do once Tom was able to care for himself.

Thanks to the generous salary Tom was paying her, she'd been able to pay for the rental of their basement suite in town until the end of January. But once this job was finished, once Tom was able to manage the stairs on his own and look after himself, she'd have to start looking for a new job.

"Mom! Mom! Come and see the tree we got," Toby called as he came racing into the kitchen twenty minutes later, his cheeks rosy, his eyes alight with excitement.

"How big is it?" she asked as she turned to smile at him.

"Mitch says it will almost reach the ceiling," Toby responded.

"That is big. Did you have fun?" she asked.

Toby nodded vigorously. "Mitch let me choose the tree, and I helped him cut it down," he told her. "That was the hard part," he added with emphasis. "Mitch did most of it," he said as his father came into the kitchen. "But I helped, didn't I?"

Abby's pulse took a giant leap as Mitch joined them. Like his son, Mitch's cheeks bore a red splash of color, and as their eyes met Abby felt her heart jolt in response. "You certainly did," Mitch acknowledged, gently ruffling his son's hair.

"Can we put the tree up and decorate it now?" Toby wanted to know.

Mitch smiled, remembering posing the exact same question the first time he'd helped his father cut down a Christmas tree. "We'll have to let it dry out for a day or two," he said, noting as he spoke that Toby's smile began to fade. "But I could sure use a hand to carry it inside," he added. "First we need to find the tree stand. It's probably upstairs in the attic in with the decorations. Want to help me look for it?"

"Okay," Toby said, brightening a little.

"And what would you say to a toboggan ride after lunch?" Mitch asked.

Toby's eyes grew as big as saucers. "Do you really have a tow...a...bog...a boggan?" He stumbled over the word.

The deep, rich sound of Mitch's laughter filled the room, sending a whisper of pleasure along her spine.

"Yes, I really have a...boggan," Mitch confirmed, amusement still humming through his voice. "It's outside in the shed. Mind you, it hasn't been used in quite some time. Still, a bit of wax should do the trick. Then we'll take it over to Bishop's Hill and give it a whirl."

"Neat-o!" Toby announced. "Where's Bishop's Hill?"

"Across the adjoining field next door and at the top of the hill. The land belongs to our neighbors, the Bishops, but at this time of year it's open to the townsfolk," Mitch explained. "Every winter when I was your age, my friends and I would take our toboggans there. It's an ideal spot. A few bushes but not too many trees."

"Want to come with us?" Toby turned to his mother.

Abby hesitated. It had been a long time since she'd ridden on a toboggan down Bishop's Hill, but she readily remembered the thrill of the ride. "Well..." she began, sorely tempted.

"Please, Mom," Toby pleaded, weakening her resolve further. "It'll be fun," he added.

"Toby's right. And besides, the toboggan runs better with three," Mitch said, determined not to let her back out this time. "Unless, of course, you're afraid," he challenged softly.

Abby met his steely gaze head-on. For some unaccountable reason he was baiting her, and while she knew she should ignore the challenge, the minute she saw the glint of mischief in the depths of his pale blue eyes she found she couldn't resist. "When are we leaving?" she asked.

"After lunch," Mitch said easily. While the trip to the Simpson farm with Toby had been an outing he wouldn't soon forget, he hadn't been able to shake the feeling that something was missing. And when Toby kept chattering about his mother, Mitch silently acknowledged that part of the joy of Christmas was sharing special moments with family and friends. And as the mother of his son, Abby was indeed family. "Come on, Toby. Let's go up in the attic and find the tree stand," he said before turning away.

As Abby mixed the ingredients to make a batch of cheese buns, she wondered if she'd been too impulsive accepting Mitch's challenge. While his initial anger on learning Toby was his son appeared to have dissipated, she felt as if she was waiting for the other shoe to fall.

Mitch cared about Toby, that much was obvious, and listening to the voices and laughter coming from the stairs, it was easy to tell that the bond between father and son was growing and deepening.

And while it wasn't exactly fair to compare Mitch to Cal, Abby couldn't ignore the fact that they'd worked in the same profession, a profession more demanding and challenging than most, a profession that left little time for the needs of a child.

Tom had spoken of his son's dedication to his job, and silently Abby reminded herself that Mitch's stay in Peachville was only temporary. On one hand Toby had a right to know the truth about Mitch; on the other Abby was fearful that knowing the truth might cause more turmoil, especially when Mitch returned to his job in Vancouver.

"Come on, Mom," Toby said as he hopped from one foot to the other waiting for Abby to put on her winter boots. They'd finished lunch half an hour before and while Toby and Mitch had gone to the shed to locate the toboggan, Abby had popped upstairs to check on Tom and make sure he'd be comfortable until they returned.

"Where's your toque?" Abby asked as she followed Toby outside.

"Right here," came the reply as Toby hauled it out of his pocket and put it on. "See the... boggan? Isn't it neat?"

Abby gazed down at the long wooden sled sitting in the snow. "Sure is," she replied, flashing him a smile, thinking that in order for three people to sit on it, they'd have to be scrunched close together.

"All set?" Mitch asked with a smile when he appeared from around the corner of the shed. He looked rugged and handsome in his burgundy ski jacket atop a pullover sweater and jeans, and Abby felt her pulse pick up speed in a response she could neither control nor ignore.

"We're ready, aren't we, Mom?" Toby smiled at his mother.

"You bet," Abby replied, tucking her gloved hands into the pockets of her green-and-white ski jacket, silently chastising herself for reacting at all.

"Let's get this show on the road," Mitch said.

Toby reached for the rope attached to the toboggan and began to pull. Mitch added his muscle and as Abby fell into step beside them, she was surprised at the feeling of happiness wrapping itself around her.

The sky was cloudless and the air was crisp and refreshingly cold as they made their way across the field adjoining Tom's property. When they reached the crest of Bishop's Hill, Abby's breath caught in her throat as she gazed across the snow-covered valley that looked like a beautiful hand-stitched quilt.

A number of families with young children and several groups of teenagers were already enjoying the snow-covered slope, and squeals of joy and laughter echoed through the air.

Toby's eyes widened in wonder as he watched several children clinging to makeshift sleds race down the relatively gentle slope. Mitch led the way to what appeared to be the starting area.

Without waiting to be told, Toby immediately dropped onto the front of the toboggan, gazing up at Abby in excitement and anticipation.

"Come on, Mom. Hop on," he instructed as he slid forward to make room for her.

Abby hesitated, but only for a second. Straddling the toboggan, she sat behind Toby, putting her arms around her son and stretching her legs out in front, as he had done. Moments later Mitch dropped onto the seat behind her.

Even through the thickness of her jacket, Abby was all too aware of his body pressed hard against hers. As his hands came around her waist, she couldn't ignore the tremor that raced along her flesh, or the heat suddenly spiraling through her veins.

"Hold on!" Mitch called out as the toboggan began to move forward and gradually pick up speed.

As the toboggan sped down the slope, Toby screeched in delight and Abby clung to her son, fearful he would slide off. The cold air stinging her cheeks was both invigorating and exhilarating, sending a rush of adrenaline through her, awakening every cell to tingling life.

She'd forgotten the electrifying sensation of hurtling downhill. As the landscape blurred into a sea of white, Mitch tightened his hold on her and she wondered if he could feel the frantic pounding of her heart.

When the toboggan slowed to a halt at the bottom of the hill, Toby leaned against Abby, tilting his head to grin up at her. "Wow! That was totally cool," he said, his eyes sparkling with joy.

"Totally," Abby said breathlessly moments before Toby struggled free of her embrace and jumped to his feet.

"Can we do that again?" Toby asked, ready and eager for the climb back to the top.

"Absolutely," Mitch answered as he reluctantly released his hold on Abby. Rising to his feet, he held out his gloved hand to her.

As Mitch tugged her to her feet she slipped on the snow and stumbled against him.

"Sorry." Abby tried to catch her breath. Glancing up, she met his gaze and for a fleeting moment she thought she saw desire flare in the depths of his pale eyes. Her heart shuddered before righting its rhythm once more.

"Mom. Mitch. Come on, you guys," Toby's urgent plea effectively cut through the tension suddenly hovering between them.

Mitch immediately spun away to grab the toboggan rope Toby held out to him, and together they began to make their way up the slope. Abby followed, telling herself over and over that nothing would have happened even if Toby hadn't been there.

On reaching the top, Toby instantly dropped onto the front of the toboggan.

"Are you coming, Mom?" he asked.

"I think I'll pass this time," Abby said, deliberately avoiding Mitch's gaze. But Mitch made no comment, climbing on behind Toby in one easy stride. They were gone in an instant and as she watched them gather speed she wasn't sure whether she was relieved or disappointed that he hadn't tried to change her mind.

As she waited for Mitch and Toby to return she chatted briefly to several acquaintances and watched three teenagers on snowboards trying out various maneuvers and trick jumps.

"Mom! Mom!"

Abby turned to see Toby with a look of such happiness on his face that she instantly felt the sting of tears in her eyes. "How was the ride?" she asked, smiling back at her son.

"Mitch and I fell off at the bottom," he told her breathlessly, laughter evident in his voice. "Then we saw Norman, he's my friend at school, remember? He's here, too. He has his very own sled and he asked if I'd like to ride down with him. Can I, Mom? Please?"

Abby glanced at Mitch. "I don't know..." she began. When he'd ridden down the slope with Mitch she hadn't worried about his well-being for a second, but all at once she was unable to squash the fear that leapt into her heart.

"I'll be careful, Mom. I promise." Toby jumped in, his blue eyes begging her for approval.

"They'll be fine," Mitch assured her as if he knew exactly what she was thinking.

Soothed by Mitch's confident tone, Abby relented. "Okay," she said, and with a grin Toby turned and scampered off to where Norman stood waiting.

"If it'll make you feel any better we can follow them down," Mitch suggested, turning the toboggan in readiness for another descent.

Abby flicked a glance to where Toby and Norman were already on their way.

"All right," she said, straddling the sled and sitting down. Before she could even think about changing her mind, Mitch hopped on behind her and in a matter of seconds they were off.

The fact that Toby was no longer sitting in front of her, his small body partially shielding hers from the icy blast, put a different slant on the ride. And a moment later when the wind's icy fingers plucked her toque from her head, Abby let out a squeal of surprise.

Shutting her eyes against the biting wind, she felt Mitch's arms tighten around her and instinctively she leaned back against his broad chest, savoring his warmth and his strength, wishing with a quiet desperation that he would hold her like this forever.

All at once the toboggan changed direction. As it veered to the right it hit something buried in the snow, bringing the toboggan to a shuddering halt and propelling them both onto the snow-covered slope. They rolled over several times before sliding to a halt at the edge of a large rhododendron bush.

Winded but unhurt, Abby opened her eyes to see Mitch on the snow beside her, his face only a few inches from hers, his expression one of grave concern.

"Are you all right? Are you hurt?" Mitch asked as he lifted himself onto his elbows.

"I'm fine," she told him a trifle breathlessly.

Reaching over, he gently brushed snow from her hair. His warm breath fanned her face and as their glances collided Abby felt her heart beat wildly. She watched, mesmerized, as his eyes darkened to a midnight blue and then her vision blurred as he closed the gap between them and tenderly touched his mouth to hers.

Mitch felt a shudder vibrate through him as Abby's mouth instantly opened beneath his in invitation. His tongue delved inside to perform an erotic dance with hers and as the kiss deepened, he tasted again those dark dusky flavors, flavors he'd never been able to forget.

Sweet, she was so damn sweet. And hot, warming him, soothing him, exciting him. Desire zipped like lightning up his spine, sending a wave of need crashing over him, sweeping him quickly to the edge of reason.

What was there about this woman that touched a chord deep within him, igniting a response he could neither ignore nor control? He couldn't seem to get enough of the taste of her, the scent of her, the feel of her.

For a moment Abby wondered if she was still riding on the toboggan. The world was spinning out of control and her heart was reeling from the sweet devastation of Mitch's kiss.

Need exploded like a flash fire inside her and she could no more resist the longing tugging at her insides than fly to the moon. Nothing had ever felt more right or more real. This was the one man, the only man who'd ever touched her heart and captured her soul.

Dear God! She loved him! Had always loved him! The startling realization, one she knew she'd been denying ever since he'd walked back into her life over a week ago, stunned her into immobility, freezing her senses and numbing her brain.

Aware of the dramatic change in her response, Mitch broke the kiss, banking the fires raging through him. As he gazed into eyes that were arousingly unfocused and heavy with desire he was at a loss to know the reason for the tears pooling in her eyes, or the look of pain shimmering in their green depths.

"Abby, what is it? What's wrong?" Mitch asked, his voice husky, his tone urgent.

"Mom! Mom!" Toby's yell, tinged with fear, shattered the silence.

Muttering under his breath, Mitch jumped to his feet and turned to greet his son, who was running through the snow toward them.

"Your mother's fine," Mitch assured him with a quick smile, though he wasn't altogether sure he was speaking the truth. For the life of him he couldn't get out of his mind the look he'd just seen in Abby's eyes. "We tumbled off the toboggan, just like you and I did, that's all," he explained as Toby came to a halt.

Pushing herself onto her elbows, Abby sat up. This time she ignored Mitch's outstretched hand and struggled to her feet unaided.

"Are you okay, Mom?" Abby heard the tremor in her son's voice and, pinning on a smile, she nodded.

"No broken bones. I'm just a bit winded, that's all," she told him, and saw the relief that flashed in her son's eyes.

"Are you sure?" he asked. "You were just lying there."

"Positive," Abby quickly answered, ignoring the ache slowly spreading through her, an ache that had nothing to do with the mishap and everything to do with the man beside her.

"Where's the toboggan?" she asked, wanting to distract Toby's attention.

"It's back there." Toby pointed to where the toboggan lay sticking out of the snow, twenty feet away.

Abby was quiet as they made the slow climb back to the top. Inside she was numb as she tried to recover from the shock of her discovery. For her the joy and fun had gone out of the day, but she encouraged Toby and Mitch to take one more foray down the slope, determined not to spoil the afternoon for Toby, or let Mitch see how deeply their kiss had affected her.

Throughout the walk back to the house she managed to keep up a bright and breezy conversation and listened intently as Toby recounted each hair-raising ride down the snowy slope.

On the pretext of wanting to get out of her wet clothes, Abby escaped to the relative sanctuary of her bedroom. Closing the door behind her, she leaned against it for support, telling herself over and over that she wasn't still in love with Mitch, that the kiss they'd shared had meant nothing at all.

But her heart stubbornly refused to listen. She loved Mitch, had never stopped loving him. Biting down on the inner softness of her mouth, she fought to stop the tears suddenly threatening to fall and wondered if she could survive having her heart broken all over again.

Chapter Nine

Abby turned off the shower, and after wrapping herself in a big bath towel sat down on her bed, wishing she could simply crawl under the covers and stay there for the rest of the afternoon and evening.

With a tired sigh she reached for a second towel and started to gently dry her hair, wondering, not for the first time, just how she was going to face Mitch. The knowledge that she loved him, had never stopped loving him, settled like a weight around her heart, and the prospect of sitting across the kitchen table making small talk and pretending that everything was right with the world seemed somehow daunting.

Her best course of action was to forget the kiss they'd shared and the revelation that had followed, but as she made her way downstairs, dressed in a navy shirt and matching stirrup pants, she knew that was much easier said than done.

To her relief she found Toby alone in the kitchen.

"Where's Mitch?" she asked before she could stop herself.

"He went upstairs to take a shower," Toby said.

He would need a new dressing for his wound. The thought jumped into Abby's mind but resolutely she shoved it aside. It had been several days since he'd asked her to look at his injury and no doubt he'd been managing to change the dressing himself.

After putting the casserole she'd made earlier into the oven, Abby set the table for dinner. When Mitch reappeared wearing jeans and a deep mauve knitted pullover, his hair still damp from the shower, Abby tried desperately to ignore the way her heart began to hammer inside her breast at the sight of him.

Throughout the meal her eyes constantly strayed toward him, drinking in his finely chiseled features, his silky black hair, the wide breadth of his shoulders and his strong, capable hands, hands that could evoke a response . . . Fool! Silently she chastised herself and the direction her thoughts had taken.

Conversation during dinner was stilted and Toby, too, seemed quieter than usual. Glancing at her son, Abby noted with some concern his flushed cheeks.

"I don't feel so good," Toby suddenly announced, pushing his plate aside.

Abby instantly reached over and put her hand on his forehead. His skin felt hot and damp and his eyes were glassy.

"I think you have a bit of a temperature, sweetie," she said, keeping her tone even.

"Do you want me to call Dr. Stone?" Mitch asked, anxiety edging his voice.

"No, that won't be necessary," Abby was quick to reply. "Toby's just overtired. A good night's rest is what he needs." She was confident she was right, knowing from experience Toby's tendency to react this way after a busy or hectic day. "Come on, darling, I'll tuck you in bed and give you a children's aspirin. That should do the trick."

Toby made no protest, a sign that he was indeed feeling out of sorts.

"Good night, Toby. Hope you feel better tomorrow," Mitch said as Abby led Toby from the room.

Once in his pajamas, Toby seemed content to climb into bed. "Will I be able to go to school tomorrow?" he wanted to know after swallowing the aspirin she gave him.

Abby nodded. "It's my guess you'll feel like your old self again in the morning," she assured him.

Toby managed a faint smile. "I hope so," he said. "'Cause tomorrow Mrs. Spracklin is collecting our letters to Santa and taking them to the post office."

"You certainly don't want to miss that, do you?" Abby responded with a smile.

Toby shook his head. "Do you think Santa will bring everything on my list?" he asked, his tone serious.

"Hmm. I suppose it depends how long your list is," Abby said as she sat on the edge of his bed.

"Not very long," Toby replied. "It's just...well...there's something special that I want...." He stopped and glanced down at his hands resting on the coverlet.

"Do you mean a new bike?" Abby gently combed a lock of his hair off his forehead.

"I do want a bike. But, well . . ." Toby's voice trailed off and he dropped his chin onto his chest.

"But what, darling?" Abby asked, surprised by his reticence.

"It's just... There's something else, something special," Toby said, and Abby's heart sank. What could he be talking about, she wondered? What was the "something special" he was referring to?

She'd been so confident that a bike had been the most important item on his list that she'd already ordered it. But now Abby wished she'd been paying more attention yesterday, when Toby had put the finishing touches to his letter to Santa.

He'd asked her for an envelope, and after handing one over she'd watched him carefully fold his letter and seal it inside. After printing To Santa in large letters across the front, he'd tucked it inside one of his schoolbooks.

"Something special, you say," Abby repeated. "I wonder what that could be?"

"It's sort of a secret," Toby said. "Just between me and Santa." He averted his gaze.

"Well, Santa reads every piece of mail, and he tries his very best to make every child's Christmas wish come true," she told him, hoping against hope that in the next few days she could somehow coax his secret out of him.

At her words Toby brightened. "Then this will be the bestest Christmas ever, just like you promised, Mom."

Abby bit back the sigh hovering on her lips. "I hope so, darling. I hope so." She bent to kiss his cheek. "Snuggle down and go to sleep. I'll be back to check on you in a little while," she said, rising from the bed. "If you need anything, just holler."

Toby nodded and closed his eyes.

Abby popped into Tom's room to collect his supper tray and after a brief chat with him, reluctantly made her way downstairs.

In the kitchen Mitch stood at the sink washing the supper dishes. The sleeves of his sweater were pushed up above his elbows, and soapsuds clung to his arms and hands as he rinsed a plate and set it in the dish rack.

An ache that was all too familiar began to spread through her, and her heart began to beat a shade too fast. It would be all too easy to buy into the fantasy that this scene was one of domestic bliss, that Mitch was her husband, that they were a real family. But much as she might wish it, the likelihood of her fantasy ever coming true was as remote as winning a lottery.

"How's Toby feeling?" Mitch asked, obviously sensing her presence.

"A little better, I think," Abby replied. "He's had quite a day, what with chopping down a Christmas tree and then going tobogganing." She kept her tone light.

"It's been quite a day all round," Mitch said, turning to meet her gaze. For a heart-stopping second Abby saw something flicker in the depths of his eyes, telling her all too clearly that he was thinking of their mishap on the slope and the resulting kiss.

Abby lowered her eyes and set Tom's dishes on the counter, aware all the while of the tension zipping through her. But much as she longed to escape upstairs to her room, her conscience wouldn't allow her to abandon her duties.

Picking up a tea towel she began to dry the dishes, and for several minutes they worked side by side in quiet efficiency, while the silence stretched between them like a rubber band ready to snap.

"Tell me about Toby." Mitch dropped the words like bombs from a plane and for a moment Abby wondered if she'd merely dreamed them, but his sideways quizzical glance told her she wasn't mistaken.

Swallowing the lump of emotion lodged in her throat, she spoke. "What do you want to know?" she asked, surprised that her voice sounded both calm and natural while inside her nerves were ajitter.

"Everything," came Mitch's husky reply, and it was all Abby could do to hold back the tears suddenly blurring her vision.

"Everything," she repeated as a deluge of guilt washed over her. For the first time she was faced with the enormity of what she had done. By not telling Mitch about the existence of his son, she'd deprived him of a great many important and unforgettable moments in the boy's life, moments that could never be repeated or recaptured.

"It's little enough to ask," Mitch observed. Rinsing off the last few pieces of cutlery, he dropped them onto the drain board. He hadn't meant to sound defensive, but ever since they'd returned from the tobogganing trip where he'd watched other families with young children partaking in the fun, he'd found himself wondering about Toby's early childhood, realizing with a pang that he'd missed out on a number of significant events in his young son's life.

"I didn't mean—" Abby abruptly broke off. Mitch was right, it was little enough to ask. The fact that he cared enough to want to know about the years he'd missed touched her deeply, and the least she could do was to recount Toby's most memorable times.

"Do you have any photographs?" Mitch asked as the water drained away.

Abby frowned. She had numerous snapshots of Toby, snapshots she'd taken at regular intervals ever since his birth, but they were all in the photo albums she kept in a box in their basement suite in Peachville.

"No, I'm afraid I don't. At least, not here," she told him. "Wait! I have some photos in my wallet," she said, remembering the professional photographs she'd had taken whenever one of the large chain stores had had a sale on children's portraits. Several wallet-sized photos came with those packages and each year she'd added an updated photo to the ones she carried around with her.

"May I see them?" Mitch asked.

"Of course. I'll be right back," Abby replied, and tossing the tea towel onto the counter she hurried from the room.

Mitch picked up the towel Abby had discarded and quickly finished drying the remaining items on the drain board. Filling the kettle from the tap, he set it on the stove, then turned to the cupboard and extracted two of his mother's favorite china teacups.

Not for the first time since his return home, he found himself wishing his mother was here. Many a night in his teens, when he'd come home from a party or a night out with his friends, he'd found her sitting in the kitchen drinking tea. She'd insisted that she wasn't waiting up for him and he'd pretended to believe her.

During those late-night sessions he'd talked to her about his dream of becoming a policeman, of setting the criminals on their heels. She'd listened attentively and offered encouragement, smiling through her tears as she told him she was behind him one hundred percent.

Those were the memories of his mother he treasured most. How he missed her and the love and warmth she'd given so generously.

As Mitch let his thoughts drift back over his own childhood he realized how fortunate he'd been to have had two loving parents, two people who'd cared deeply about each other and about him. Silently he acknowledged that his father had played an equally important role in his life, teaching him and guiding him through those years, yet always giving him the room to grow and learn from his own mistakes.

The only thing he and his father had never quite seen eye-to-eye about had been Mitch's choice of career. Tom had assumed his son would follow in his footsteps, just as he had followed in his father's, and after learning the ropes of how to run a retail business, he and Mitch would work side by side at Tennyson's, until the time came for Tom to retire.

His mother had been his ally, understanding his need to venture out into the world and make it on his own. Though Mitch knew his father was proud of him, Tom had never really understood or approved of the path Mitch had chosen, a path his father believed had been responsible for turning Mitch into an unfeeling, uncaring man. What other reason could there be for a son to turn his back on his family during a time of need?

Silently he acknowledged that he could have, and probably should have, handled in a better way the situation that had arisen as a result of his mother's terminal illness. Perhaps if he'd taken an extended leave of absence, been there for his father, the resulting estrangement wouldn't have happened.

But instead Mitch had volunteered for an assignment, thinking that by burying himself in his work he'd avoid the pain of watching his adored mother slowly and painfully lose the battle for her life.

For the first time Mitch faced the painful realization that like his father, he, too, had been in a state of denial, and his decision to throw himself back into his work after her death had merely compounded the problem, allowing the gap growing between him and his father to widen.

But that wasn't all. There had been other victims, innocent victims: Abby, who'd found him wandering like a lost soul and taken him in, giving of herself unselfishly, saving his sanity; and Toby, the child they'd created that night, a night he'd never been able to forget.

He'd made a botch of things, pure and simple, but there was still time to salvage something from the wreckage. Toby was his son, his own flesh and blood, and that fact alone shed a new and totally different light on things, shifting his perception of his relationship with his father and changing his own perspective on life.

But Mitch knew that whatever decision he made regarding the future, it wasn't a decision to be taken lightly or without some considerable thought, not when Toby's welfare and happiness were the prime concern.

"I'm sorry about the wait," Abby said as she reentered the kitchen. "Your father wanted me to look for a book he thought was in his bookcase. Here are the photographs." She spread on the counter the half-dozen pictures she'd extracted from her wallet.

"Thanks," Mitch said, glancing quickly from one photo to the next.

"I wrote on the back the date and Toby's age at the time each picture was taken," she volunteered.

"I see," Mitch responded, turning over first one picture then another. "He was a beautiful baby," he murmured as he studied the photograph taken a few days after Toby's birth.

"Yes ... yes, he was," Abby agreed. It seemed like only yesterday that the doctor had told her she had a son, then handed her the tiny miracle. "He was just a year old in that one," she said as Mitch gently fingered the second photo.

"He doesn't look very happy," Mitch commented wryly.

"No," Abby said. "Toby never liked having to sit still. From the minute he learned to walk when he was eleven months old, I had my hands full. That's because he never walked anywhere—he ran, and always at breakneck speed."

A smile started to curl at the corners of Mitch's mouth, sending a shiver of awareness chasing through her. "My mother was known to voice a similar complaint about me. She was forever accusing me of having ants in my pants," he told her, his smile widening. "What about this one?" He pointed to the photograph of Toby at age two.

For almost an hour Abby related stories and anecdotes about Toby, from the time at the age of three he'd hidden in a closet while playing hide-and-seek with some friends and promptly fallen asleep, to the time only last year when she'd had to take him to Emergency due to a frighteningly high fever that had turned out to herald a case of tonsillitis.

As she talked, Mitch poured tea into the cups and invited her to sit at the kitchen table. He listened intently, interrupting her on occasion to ask questions or to recount a story or a particular memory from his own childhood.

"I'd better check on Toby," Abby said, rising from the table. "I think I'll call it a night," she added, noting with some surprise that it was almost eleven.

"Hmm?" Mitch, who for the past five minutes had been staring in silence at the photographs spread in front of him, dragged his gaze away, still marveling at the miracle that was his son. "Oh...sure," he said. "And Abby...thanks."

Abby heard the warmth and appreciation in his voice and not for the first time wondered what would have happened if she hadn't listened to Cal, if she had contacted Mitch. Would things have been different? It was a question she could never know the answer to. "You can keep those. I have lots more at my apartment," she offered.

"Maybe I could see those sometime," Mitch said.

"Of course," Abby replied before withdrawing.

Mitch dropped his gaze once again to the photographs. Abby's descriptive and mostly amusing stories about Toby had brought his son's early years to vivid life, but Mitch had noticed that she'd never once mentioned Cal or included him in any of the tales, almost as if Roberts had played no part in Toby's life at all.

On reflection, the fact that Roberts had told Toby he wasn't his real father was a strong indication that Roberts had cared little for the boy, and Mitch wondered anew if the reason for Cal's cruel and heartless disclosure had had something to do with the fact that he'd known Mitch was Toby's real father.

All in all, Toby had turned out exceptionally well and the credit, Mitch felt sure, belonged solely to Abby. That she put her son's welfare first and foremost was obvious, and Mitch admired her for that, and for the warmth and compassion that were such an integral part of her. Those were the qualities that had drawn him to her that night seven years ago, and those were the qualities that drew him to her now.

She stirred his senses as no other woman ever had. But that wasn't all. There was something about her, something less easy to define. Suddenly an idea struck him, an idea that set both his heart and mind racing. He'd have to think it through, evaluate the pros and cons, but irrational and impulsive as it seemed, he knew it was the perfect solution. All he had to do was convince Abby.

As Abby had predicted, Toby felt as right as rain the next morning, happily heading off to catch the school bus, his letter to Santa tucked safely in his bag. Mitch had already left for the market and as she climbed the stairs to collect Tom's breakfast tray, Abby wondered if it might be worth calling her son's teacher to ask if she'd take a peek at Toby's letter to Santa and report her findings.

Upstairs she found Tom making his way down the hall with the aid of the walker. "If you keep this up, you'll be able to go tobogganing with Mitch and Toby next weekend," she teased as she caught up with him.

Tom chuckled. "Inviting as that idea sounds, I think my days of tobogganing are over," he said.

While Tom continued to walk the length of the hall and back, Abby took the opportunity to change his bedding and tidy his bedroom.

"Abby," Tom said half an hour later when he was back in bed once more, "would you mind having a look downstairs on the shelves in the living room for that book I was looking for last night? It's called *The Canadian Connection*. It's about the Canadian troops and their part in the Second World War. It's a particular favorite of mine and I have a yen to reread it."

"Sure, I'll check," she replied.

After turning on the washing machine, Abby headed to the living room. She scanned the bookshelves for the missing book, to no avail. As she pondered the problem, she wondered if perhaps there was a bookshelf in the master bedroom, the bedroom Tom had shared with his wife, Rose.

Telling herself that if she found the missing book she could always say it had been on the shelf in the living room, Abby decided to take a chance.

As she opened the door to the master bedroom, she felt a pang of guilt at intruding where Tom had specifically asked her not to, but resolutely she pushed those thoughts aside. She flicked the light switch, but nothing happened, and silently she concluded that the light bulbs in the ceiling fixture had burned out.

Inside, the room was dark and dreary and the air felt heavy and oppressive. Abby quickly crossed the carpeted floor to the nearest window, throwing open the heavy drapes. A shaft of sunlight instantly brightened the room to reveal a queen-size bed covered with a white drop cloth. All the remaining pieces of furniture were also hidden beneath equally large dustcovers.

Moving to the second window, Abby opened those drapes, letting in another ray of light and sunshine. After a quick look around Abby located what she thought was a bookcase, against the wall next to the bed.

Dust specks danced in the bright sunlight as she gently tugged the cloth free. She smiled triumphantly when she saw the mahogany bookshelf with row upon row of books, some of them leather bound. She ran her eyes quickly down the shelves and several titles caught her eye, but before she could look more closely she suddenly started to sneeze.

A little fresh air would do the trick, she thought. The window lock gave way at the third try and after pushing it open several inches Abby returned to the bookshelf. A lover of books herself, she quickly became distracted, lingering over familiar titles and browsing through others whose authors she recognized.

Although she wasn't entirely positive, she thought a number of the books were first editions, and when her eyes lit on the title *Little Women* by Louisa May Alcott, she could no more pass it by than fly to the moon.

Making herself more comfortable on the carpeted floor, she was soon reacquainting herself with the unforgettable characters.

"Abby? Are you in here?"

At the sound of Tom's voice Abby's head snapped up and she dropped the book onto the carpet. Jumping to her feet, she stared in astonishment at Tom, standing in the doorway.

"Tom? How did you...? I'm sorry. I thought... I'm sorry." She ground to a halt, feeling her face grow warm as conflicting emotions of guilt, surprise and relief all warred within her. Guilt for having been caught where she had no right to be, surprise because Tom had tackled the stairs on his own and relief that he'd negotiated them safely and made his way to the bedroom without the help of the walker.

"I was calling you," Tom said almost absently. "And when you didn't reply I got a bit worried." He took another small step into the room.

Abby was at his side in an instant. "I didn't hear you, Tom. I'm sorry," she apologized again, beginning to sound like a broken record. "I know I shouldn't have come in here. I hope you'll forgive me, but I thought I might find the book you wanted. Are you all right? Would you like to sit down?"

"There's an armchair under that cloth," he told her, nodding to where the outline of a chair could be seen.

Abby moved to uncover the armchair, a lovely Queen Anne style, upholstered in a beautiful floral brocade. As Tom lowered himself into it, his gaze slowly scanned the room. Abby held her breath.

"My Rose loved this room," Tom said at last, his voice husky with emotion.

"I can understand why. It's beautiful," Abby responded, her tone sincere, aware even if Tom wasn't that he'd just taken a giant step toward coming to terms with the loss of his wife.

"She chose every piece of furniture herself, and the paint and wallpaper," he told her. "She was so proud of this room." Abby's heart ached for him when she saw the glint of tears in his eyes.

"Then it seems such a shame to shut it away and not enjoy it," she said softly.

Tom made no reply and Abby watched as his gaze traveled around the room once more, his hands gently caressing the upholstered arm of the chair. Thinking it would be wise to leave him alone with his memories for a while, Abby silently withdrew and closed the door.

As she hurried to collect the walker Tom had abandoned at the top of the stairs, she wished Mitch had picked up the wheelchair from the hospital. If Tom should decide to come downstairs each day, the wheelchair would allow him to move around on the main floor without tiring himself out too much.

Perhaps she should call Mitch and ask him to stop by the hospital. After leaving the walker outside the bedroom door in case Tom should need it, Abby returned to the kitchen and dialed the number for the store.

"Tennyson's Market. Mitch Tennyson speaking."

As Mitch's deep voice throbbed in her ear, a frisson of awareness danced across her nerve endings. "Ah...Mitch, it's Abby," she said, glad that her voice at least sounded normal.

"Abby? What is it? What's wrong?" he asked. "Is it my father? Is he all right?" Mitch's urgent barrage of questions cut through her mental haze.

"Nothing's wrong. Tom's fine," Abby quickly reassured him. "In fact, he's better than fine. He came downstairs by himself this morning."

"He what?" Surprise echoed through Mitch's voice.

"He came downstairs. He's here now," Abby reaffirmed.

"In the kitchen?" Mitch asked.

"No," she replied. "You probably aren't going to believe this, either, but he's in the master bedroom."

The silence on the other end of the line told her Mitch was indeed taken aback by the news. "And he's all right...I mean, really all right?"

Abby heard and understood the deeper meaning behind the question. "Yes, I think so," she responded. "I'll fill you in later, but right now he's sitting in an armchair in the bedroom."

"That's wonderful," Mitch said. "Progress indeed. Thanks for letting me know."

"Mitch, wait." Abby hurried on. "I was thinking it might be a good idea if you went by the hospital and picked up the wheelchair. If Tom decides to make a habit of this, coming downstairs I mean, the wheelchair would be a big help."

"You're right. I'll stop by the hospital before I head home."

"Thanks," Abby replied.

"Oh, Abby." It was Mitch's turn to delay breaking the connection. "There's something I want to discuss with you...about Toby," he said.

Abby felt her pulse rocket out of control. "You've made a decision." The words were a comment, not a question.

"Yes, I've made a decision," Mitch acknowledged. "I'd like to talk to you about it tonight, after supper. Alone. Is that okay?"

Abby swallowed convulsively, trying to alleviate the sudden dryness in her throat. "Fine," she managed to say, though her voice sounded far away.

"Good," Mitch responded. "I'll see you later," he added before hanging up.

Abby slowly replaced the receiver. Her heart was beating a frantic tattoo in her breast and she had to fight down the panic threatening to overwhelm her. She refused to speculate about what Mitch's decision might be. She would know soon enough. She would know tonight.

Resolutely she turned her thoughts away from Mitch. Curious and a little concerned about Tom, Abby made her way to the master bedroom and entered after knocking lightly on the door.

Tom sat in the chair where she'd left him. He glanced up when she entered and even managed a smile. It was obvious from the books and photo albums spread out on the bed in front of him that he'd been making a trip down memory lane.

"Tom, is everything all right?" she asked.

"I'm fine," Tom said. "Just fine. I should have done this years ago." He sighed.

"Done what?" Abby asked, moving to sit opposite him on the edge of the bed.

"Come in here," he replied. "But I just couldn't bear to." His voice was thick with suppressed emotion. "And as time passed I kept putting it off, telling myself I would, one day."

"You weren't ready," Abby said.

"I still miss her, you know," he said softly.

"I know," Abby replied. Reaching out, she covered his hand with one of her own.

He met her gaze and smiled. "I should have listened to Mitch. I should have brought Rose home," Tom said. "I was too darned stubborn—" He broke off.

Abby felt her heart swell with sympathy and understanding. "You did what you thought was best," she said, wanting to comfort him, to ease his burden.

"But I let her down in the end." Tom's voice was little more than a whisper, and she could hear the pain and the anguish, but she kept silent, sensing that Tom simply needed to talk, needed someone to listen. "I wasn't with her, you see," he went on, staring straight ahead. "When she died, I mean." He took a deep breath before continuing. "Up until that night I'd been sitting by her bedside practically round the clock, catching a nap here and there, leaving her side for a few minutes now and then. But on the night my Rose died, I let her down. I wasn't there. And I still can't bear the thought that she died alone." He came to a halt and closed his eyes.

"Rose didn't die alone, Tom. Mitch was there," Abby said softly, hoping this knowledge would ease his pain.

Tom's eyes flew open and he met her gaze. "That's what he said, but no one saw him, not me or any of the nurses."

"Mitch was there. He wasn't lying," Abby said. "I saw him. I was there, too." She noted the flicker of hope in the depths of his eyes. "It was around one o'clock in the morning. I was going off duty when I ran into Mitch wandering aimlessly down one of the hospital corridors," she explained. "He was emotionally distraught and very upset. I knew your wife was a patient, and it wasn't difficult to figure out what had happened. He looked totally devastated, and I didn't like to just leave him there. I invited him back to my apartment." She stopped, feeling it was unnecessary to say more.

"Then she wasn't alone." The relief in his voice was palpable, the look on his face almost joyful. But after a brief moment his expression grew thoughtful. "I guess I just didn't want to believe Mitch. I felt guilty...guilty that I wasn't the one with her when she died." Tom stopped and drew a steadying breath. "I failed her," he added in a voice heavy with sadness.

"You didn't fail her, Tom." Abby squeezed his hand. "Your wife knew how very much you loved her. Don't you think it's time you forgave yourself and made peace with your son?" she urged gently. "Don't you think Rose would want that?"

Tom held her gaze for a long moment. "You're right. It is time."

Abby smiled. "I'm going to warm up some tomato soup for lunch. Why don't you join me in the kitchen when you're ready? The walker's right outside. I'll get it." She retrieved the walker and set it near Tom's chair. "Take your time, there's no hurry," she added before withdrawing once more.

In the kitchen Abby busied herself making grilled cheese sandwiches to accompany the soup. That Tom was finally coming to terms with his grief and was willing to make peace with Mitch warmed her heart, but while she was pleased at the prospect of a father-and-son reconciliation, she was still apprehensive about the decision Mitch had made concerning their son.

But she would know in a matter of hours. And all she could hope for was that she could accept his decision and live with it.

Chapter Ten

Tom joined Abby in the kitchen and she could see by his pale features that his sojourn downstairs had taken its toll, both physically and emotionally.

"You look tired, Tom," she said as she settled him into a chair at the table.

"I am tired," he acknowledged. "Too tired to try the stairs, I'm afraid."

"It will only take me a few minutes to put clean bedding on the bed in the master bedroom. You could take a nap in there," she suggested, but even as she voiced the suggestion Abby wondered if she was pushing things.

"But you just finished changing the bed upstairs," Tom protested.

The fact that he hadn't instantly dismissed her idea gave her the encouragement she needed. "Making beds is one of the first things a nurse learns during practical training," she told him easily. "I think I could tuck hospital corners in my sleep." She grinned. "You eat lunch, and I'll put clean sheets on the bed and give the room a once-over. What do you say?"

Tom hesitated, but only for a moment. "I say you're a treasure," he said, his tone sincere.

"Flattery will get you everywhere," Abby returned, warmed by his words.

"But what about your lunch?" Tom asked when she sat a bowl of hot soup together with a grilled cheese sandwich in front of him.

"I'll have it later," she assured him.

In the master bedroom Abby removed the dust cloths and carefully rolled them up, trying to minimize the amount of dust that escaped. While the room needed a thorough cleaning, she felt it was much more important that the progress Tom had made not be jeopardized.

To air the room quickly she opened both windows to the maximum, then proceeded to gather the books and albums from the bed and remove its dustcover. Underneath she found a handmade quilted bedspread that took her breath away. So intricate was the pattern, so beautiful the design, Abby wondered if Rose Tennyson had sewn the quilt herself.

In the linen closet in the hall Abby found a mattress cover and several sets of sheets in lovely pastel shades that matched the colorful wallpaper on the wall behind the bed.

Once the bed was made up, Abby retrieved Tom's pillows from the room upstairs. The vacuum cleaner brought life back to the carpet and after running a duster over the furniture, including the windowsills and the fireplace mantel, Abby closed the windows and lit the gas fire in the fireplace.

"Abby, you've done wonders," Tom said a short time later when she ushered him into the bedroom.

"It's still a little cool in here," she warned.

"The fire will soon chase away the chill," Tom said as he sat down on the edge of the bed. "Rose wanted me to put in a wood-burning fireplace, but I convinced her that gas would be cleaner and better, not to mention easier on the carpet." He smiled.

Abby smiled, too. "I'll leave you to it," she said.

"Abby..." Tom said, bringing her to a halt at the door. "Thanks... for everything."

Returning to the kitchen, Abby reheated a bowl of soup for herself, thinking that since Mitch's arrival a week ago a change had come over everyone. Not only had his presence jolted Tom from the depression he'd been sinking into, but his friendly, easygoing charm had helped boost Toby's confidence and given her own heart a wake-up call.

That he would be missed when the time came for him to return to his job in Vancouver was an understatement, and silently Abby hoped Tom would soon make the move toward a reconciliation with his son.

For Toby she could only pray that the decision Mitch had reached would include making both time and room in his life for his son.

After clearing the dishes Abby began to prepare the evening meal. When she heard the front door open a short time later she glanced at the clock, thinking it was too early for the school bus to have dropped Toby off.

"We're home!" Toby, still wearing his jacket and boots, came running into the kitchen.

"Toby! Why are you home early?" Abby asked, wiping her wet hands on a towel.

"Mitch picked me up from school and gave me a ride home," he announced cheerfully.

"Mitch did?" Abby repeated, surprised and pleased at the gesture.

"I passed by the school after I collected the wheelchair at the hospital," Mitch explained as he joined them in the kitchen. "When I saw the kids coming out, I thought I'd treat Toby to a ride home."

"I see," Abby said, trying to ignore the way her pulse had picked up speed at the sight of him.

"Where's my father?" Mitch asked.

"Taking a nap," Abby replied.

"You don't mean... He didn't tackle the stairs?" Mitch began.

"No, he's in the master bedroom," she quickly explained.

"Did Mr. Tom really come downstairs by himself?" Toby asked.

"Yes, he did," Abby answered with a smile. "And if he keeps making progress like this it won't be long before he'll be able to manage on his own."

At her words, Toby's face fell. "Does that mean he won't need us anymore? That we'll have to leave?" The anxiety and distress evident on her son's face and in his voice caught Abby off guard and a pain clutched at her heart at his reaction.

That he'd so quickly become attached to Tom and to the house where they'd been living was understandable, but she'd failed to realize just how much Toby had come to depend on the stability their current situation had provided.

She knew he enjoyed the fact that she was always available to him when he came home from school and on weekends, circumstances that had happened much less frequently when she'd been working shifts at the hospital.

"I wouldn't worry about that just yet," Mitch said, coming to her rescue. "When I talked to Dr. Stone today, he told me it will probably be another month or maybe more before Mr. Tom is able to look after himself."

"Really?" Toby's expression instantly brightened.

"Really," Mitch assured him with a smile.

Toby visibly relaxed. "It's not that I don't want Mr. Tom to get better or anything," Toby said, obviously feeling he needed to explain. "It's just...well, I like living here with Mr. Tom and my mom, and you, too...and I like taking the bus to school and I like..."

"Toby." Abby cut off the flow. "Darling, I'm glad you like it here, but we will have to leave when Mr. Tom is better," she reminded him, hating to rain on his parade but knowing she couldn't let Toby think their stay was an indefinite one. "Go and take your coat and boots off, please," she urged gently. "Then you can help me with supper."

With a beleaguered sigh, Toby nodded and made his way from the kitchen. Abby turned to Mitch. "We'll have to leave sometime," she asserted, trying not to sound defensive.

"That's one of the things I want to talk to you about," Mitch said.

At his words Abby's heart somersaulted in stunned surprise, but before she could ask the question suddenly buzzing inside her head Mitch hurried on. "Not now. This isn't the time." There was more than a hint of exasperation in his voice. "I'd better bring in the wheelchair and take it through to him," he continued. "Is he still napping?"

"I don't know," Abby replied, still puzzled by his comment. But Mitch was right. This wasn't the time. "After you bring in the wheelchair, why don't you take him a cup of tea and find out?" she suggested, thinking it would afford Tom a golden opportunity to talk with Mitch and perhaps settle their differences.

"Good idea. I'll be right back," he said.

While Mitch brought in the wheelchair, Abby prepared a tray for Tom, adding an extra cup for Mitch.

Toby had already rejoined her in the kitchen and was sitting at the table munching on cookies and drinking hot chocolate when Mitch reappeared. "Can I come with you to see Mr. Tom?" Toby asked.

"I need you to give me a hand with supper, Toby." Abby quickly intervened, drawing a curious glance from Mitch.

Toby groaned. "Do I have to?"

"Yes, you have to," she replied firmly.

Toby looked sullen but he knew better than to argue.

"Hey, squirt. The Christmas tree should be dry now. Want to help decorate it after supper?" Mitch asked, wanting to put a smile back on his son's face and wondering why Abby seemed intent on ensuring he have time alone with his father.

"Okay." Toby's smile blossomed.

"Great," Mitch said before making his way from the room.

"Mom, can I go and tell Mitch and Mr. Tom supper's ready?" Toby asked for the third time in as many minutes.

Abby smiled and shook her head. She was equally anxious to find out how Mitch had fared with his father, but she was also reluctant to intrude. Almost an hour had passed since Mitch had walked out of the kitchen carrying the tea tray—an hour of waiting, wondering and worrying.

It had been difficult enough to keep Toby occupied during that time, but she'd managed by coaxing him into giving her a hand, first to peel potatoes and then when they were cooked, to mash them for a topping for the meat-and-vegetable pie she'd made earlier.

"Give them a few more minutes," she said. "By the way, I forgot to ask. Did you get your letter mailed off to Santa?" she asked, hoping to distract him.

"Yes," Toby replied. "Mrs. Spracklin took our whole class to the post office just before lunch break."

"I don't remember signing a permission slip," Abby commented with a frown, knowing the school had strict rules about such things.

"You signed it last month," he said. "That's when we were supposed to go on the field trip to the post office, remember? But Mrs. Spracklin was sick and she had to, ah...poned it—"

"Postpone it, you mean," Abby corrected, recalling now that Toby was right.

"Postpone it," Toby repeated. "So we went today instead."

"Did you have fun?" she asked.

Toby nodded. "We saw some mailmen sorting out their mail and putting it into little boxes for the different streets," he said. "And the man in charge showed us the sack of letters waiting to go to Santa at the North Pole. The man said Santa usually sends his elves to pick them up. But we didn't see any elves," he added, sounding a little disappointed.

"Elves? Did you say elves?" Tom asked as Mitch wheeled him into the kitchen.

"Yeah. Hi, Mr. Tom," Toby said brightly.

Abby turned, anxious to see Tom's and Mitch's expressions. Both men appeared relaxed with no signs of tension.

"Your timing is perfect," Abby observed. "I was just about to put dinner on the table."

"Tell me about those elves, Toby," Tom said as Mitch maneuvered the wheelchair up to the table.

"I'll give Abby a hand," Mitch offered.

"That's okay. I can manage," Abby quickly assured him, but he was already at her side.

"Thanks," Mitch murmured, softly enough for only Abby to hear.

She felt his breath on her cheek, and a ripple of awareness shimmied down her spine as she darted him a startled look. "What for?" she asked as she put the buns into a basket, keeping her voice low and hoping he wouldn't notice that her hands were trembling.

"For talking to my father," he replied huskily. "You're quite a miracle worker."

"All I did was tell him you were at the hospital that night," Abby whispered, trying to make light of her role.

"Mom!" Toby's shout caught their attention and they both turned. "I spilt my milk. I'm sorry."

"No problem," Abby quickly assured him, glad of the rather timely interruption. Grabbing a cloth from the sink, she cleaned up the spill. A few minutes later, as she took her seat at the table, she wished she had a camera to record the three generations of Tennyson men.

Later, after the supper dishes had been cleared, Abby was again wishing she had her camera as she watched Toby help his father string Christmas lights around the tree. Glancing at Tom sitting near the fireplace, Abby noticed the shimmer of tears in the old man's eyes and felt sure he was remembering other Christmases years ago with his wife, Rose.

"Abby, why don't you put on some Christmas music?" Mitch suggested as he reached up to join a second strand of lights to the first.

"Good idea," Tom said. "You'll find the records in the cabinet on your right. We always put Rose in charge of the music," Tom went on almost to himself.

"And a good job she did, too," Mitch said, flashing a smile at his father, a smile edged with sadness.

"She did indeed. She did indeed," Tom responded, and Abby watched father and son exchange a meaningful look, a look of love, acceptance and understanding.

Abby blinked back tears as she pulled the records from the cabinet. She chose one of her own favorites from the collection and in a matter of minutes the living room was filled with the music of Christmas.

As Toby pulled decorations from various boxes, Tom began to recount stories of Christmases past. Mitch interrupted now and then to argue a detail or add a memory of his own. Warmth, love and laughter echoed through the room, and Abby knew she would treasure these moments of an evening she wouldn't soon forget.

The decorating completed, Abby watched Toby, his eyes sparkling with excitement, proudly switch on the tree lights. Swallowing the lump of emotion suddenly lodged in her throat, Abby joined Tom in applauding Toby's and Mitch's efforts.

Turning away, she closed her eyes and silently made a wish.

"Penny for your thoughts." Mitch's deep tones coming from directly behind her drew a gasp of surprise from Abby, and it was all she could do to steady her racing heart and find her voice.

"If I tell you, it won't come true," she managed to say and watched in fascination as his mouth curled into a knowing smile.

"I thought that only applied to wishes," Mitch observed, a hint of humor in his voice now. "I've heard it said you should be careful what you wish for. You just might get it." His gaze was intent on hers, almost as if he was trying to see inside her soul.

If only... Abby thought wistfully, and felt her body begin to sway toward him, drawn by a force older than time. If only... she thought again as a need tugged insistently at her insides, undermining her will to resist.

"Look what I found." Toby's voice cut through the haze of desire threatening to overwhelm her, and Abby instantly backed away, berating herself for her weakness.

"What did you find?" she asked, her voice trembling just a little as she crouched to Toby's level, telling herself she was grateful for her son's intervention, which had prevented her from making a colossal fool of herself.

"It's a Christmas stocking," Toby said. "See?" He held it out to her.

Abby accepted the large stocking, made from a dark green quilted material, noting with a smile the two elves, one on either side, each wearing red Santa suits and hats, carrying brightly colored packages to the top of the stocking.

"Would you look at that," Tom said with a chuckle. "Mitch's mother sewed that for him," he told Toby as he maneuvered the wheelchair a little closer.

"She did?" Toby replied, and glanced up at his father for confirmation.

"Yes, she did," Mitch answered, his voice thick with emotion.

"Wow," Toby said. "The elves must be Santa's helpers." He touched one, then the other. "They look really neat. And I bet it holds a lot."

Tom chuckled again. "That's exactly what Mitch said when his mother gave it to him," he explained.

"I sure wish I had a big stocking like that to hang up on Christmas Eve." Toby's tone was wistful.

"You do have a stocking," Abby scolded gently.

"But it's not here—it's at the apartment. And it's not as big as this one," Toby was quick to point out.

Mitch crouched to Toby's level and, taking the stocking from Abby, handed it to his son. "Then I insist you use this one. In fact, you can have it for your very own," he said.

"Really? Do you mean it?" Toby asked, eyes wide and sparkling like the sun on the ocean.

"Absolutely," Mitch replied, feeling his heart melt at the look of joy that appeared on his son's face.

"Wow! Thanks," Toby said before throwing himself at his father and giving him a hug.

Stunned by the spontaneous show of affection, Mitch almost lost his balance. As his arms closed around Toby's small frame, a feeling of love such as he'd never known before enveloped him. Tears suddenly stung his eyes and a lump of emotion lodged in his throat, making it impossible for him to speak.

He didn't want to let go, didn't want the moment to end, unable to believe the depth of his feelings for this child who was his own flesh and blood. Slowly Mitch relaxed his hold on Toby, struggling to regain control, immeasurably moved by the embrace.

"I had to put in a special hook so Mitch could hang it up," Tom said. "It's still there. See?" He pointed it out, effectively distracting Toby's attention.

"Cool!" Toby exclaimed, moving in for a closer look.

"Well . . . I don't know about you folks," Tom went on, "but I've had enough excitement for one day. I'm off to bed." He sighed.

"I'll give you a hand, Dad," Mitch offered, moving to stand behind his father. "I assume you're staying downstairs."

"It seems like the practical thing to do," Tom answered. "Good night, Abby, Toby. See you in the morning."

"Night, Mr. Tom," Toby said.

"Good night," Abby responded. "Come on, Toby. You have school tomorrow. It's time you got ready for bed, too."

Toby didn't protest. Still clutching the Christmas stocking, he fell into step behind Mitch, joining the small procession making its way from the living room.

Upstairs Abby tidied her son's room wile Toby washed his face and hands and brushed his teeth.

"I wish we could stay here forever," Toby said as he climbed into bed.

Abby bit back a sigh. "I know you do, darling," she acknowledged. "But we can't."

"It was sure nice of Mitch to give me his stocking," Toby said, glancing at the stocking lying across the foot of his bed.

"Yes, it was," Abby replied, thinking that as she'd watched Toby throw himself into Mitch's arms, revealing the deepening level of trust and affection he felt for the man who was his father, she'd felt as if her heart was slowly being squeezed in a vise.

"Do you like Mitch?" Toby suddenly asked, his blue eyes so like his father's gazing directly into hers.

Surprised and a bit flustered by the question, Abby felt her face grow warm. "Yes, I like Mitch," she said after a moment's hesitation.

"Me, too," Toby announced in heartfelt tones. "I wish—"

"No more wishes tonight." Abby quickly cut in as she bent to kiss Toby, almost sure he'd been about to say that he wished Mitch was his father. "Good night, darling," she murmured as she closed the door behind her.

Downstairs she made her way to the living room, intending to switch off the tree lights and tidy the boxes left strewn around the room. But at the sight of Mitch standing in front of the bay window, his tall lean body silhouetted against the night sky, everything was forgotten. Her breath caught in her throat and her heart started to hammer against her breastbone, as if it was trying to escape.

"Mitch?" His name came out in a throaty whisper.

Mitch spun around as if she'd startled him. "There you are," he said, taking a step toward her. "Is Toby asleep?"

"Not yet," Abby replied, coming to a halt in front of the fireplace. "You said you wanted to talk to me," she went on.

"Yes. Yes, I do," Mitch replied. For the past five minutes he'd been rehearsing what he wanted to say, but somehow now that Abby was here he felt more than a bit nervous. "Sit down," he said, closing the gap between them.

"I'd rather stand," Abby responded, trying to hide her apprehension and ignore the erratic way her pulse was behaving. He was only a few feet away, close enough to touch. A shiver of awareness zipped down her spine and she had to curl her fingers into tight fists in order to curb the urge to reach out and trace the smooth line of his jaw.

"I'll get right to the point," he began. "I think we should get married."

Abby blinked in astonishment, staring at Mitch as if he'd suddenly sprouted a pair of horns. She opened her mouth to speak but no words came. She swallowed convulsively and tried again. "Wha... What did you just say?" she managed at last, sure she was dreaming. She had to be.

"I said I think we should get married," Mitch repeated, more than a hint of irritation in his voice.

"You can't be serious," Abby said, disbelief in every syllable.

Mitch bristled at her tone. "I'm very serious," he responded, feeling his anger rise. "It's the only solution that makes any sense."

Shock dissolved into a deep and profound sadness. It was all Abby could do to meet his gaze, so intense was the pain stabbing at her heart. "But surely... I mean... don't you think that's rather a drastic measure?" she said, searching his face for an emotion, any emotion, but seeing only an icy calm.

"Did you think it was a drastic measure seven years ago when Roberts suggested you marry him?" Mitch countered, angry at her response and wishing now he'd eased into the subject of marriage instead of taking such a direct approach.

Any doubts he'd had about this decision had vanished the moment he'd held Toby in his arms. He wanted desperately to be a father to his son, wanted to be a part of the boy's life, to spend time with him and make up for all the years he'd missed.

"That was different," Abby replied. Seven years ago she'd been pregnant, alone and very vulnerable.

"Not entirely," Mitch said, keeping his tone even, silently acknowledging that by different she undoubtedly meant that her marriage to Roberts had been a marriage based on love and not characterized as a solution. "The similarity lies in that your child needed a father. He still needs a father... he needs his *real* father. He needs *me*," Mitch went on, a hint of desperation drifting into his tone.

Abby flinched inwardly. Mitch was right. Toby needed a positive male influence in his life, a role model, and who better than the man who was his real father? And she'd been wrong when she'd said this situation was different. Cal's offer of marriage seven years ago had also been presented as the solution to a problem. There had been no mention of love then, just as there was none now.

If only. If only. The words played over and over in her head like a broken record. If only Mitch loved her as much as she loved him, then her answer would have been a resounding yes.

"We could make it work." Mitch was talking again, cutting through her wayward thoughts. "I know we could make it work," he repeated.

"How?" she asked. "I couldn't take Toby back to Vancouver. He likes it here. We both do," Abby told him.

"Who said anything about going back to Vancouver?" Mitch inquired. "I'll quit my job and take over for my father at the store. It's time he retired. You heard what Dr. Stone said. And it's always been my father's dream to one day pass the store on to me, just as it was passed from his father. It's what he's always wanted."

"And what about you, Mitch? What do you want?" The question was out before she could prevent it. She was under the impression that Mitch loved working with the Vancouver police. From what Tom had told her, Mitch was dedicated to his chosen career, with a dedication that had been responsible for the friction between them.

"I want my son," Mitch said harshly. "And as far as I'm concerned a marriage between us is the simplest and best way to achieve that goal. Surely you can see that."

At his words, Abby's hopes and dreams disintegrated. "What about me?" she asked in a throaty whisper, fighting back tears. "What about what I want?" She hated it that he regarded her as nothing more than a means to an end, that marriage to her simply meant unlimited access to Toby.

"If you're asking if our marriage will be a real one, let me assure you here and now it will be real, in every sense of the word. This should convince you," he added, and with lightning speed he reached out and hauled her, none too gently, into his arms.

The anger, the pain, the anguish evaporated like steam from a kettle as Abby responded to his kiss with a hunger that shook her. This was what she wanted. This was what she needed. This was where she wanted to be, here in his arms, forever.

Only in Mitch's arms did she feel truly alive, as his kiss awakened every nerve, every cell to quivering life. She couldn't seem to get enough of the taste of him, the scent of him, the feel of him as his tongue plundered and probed, inciting a need she could neither control nor ignore.

Her heart was thundering in her breast like a herd of wild horses racing across the plains, and when his mouth left hers she suddenly felt lost and strangely bereft. Lifting her gaze to meet his, she glimpsed the raw desire shimmering in the depths of his eyes and gloried in the knowledge that he, too, was affected by the kiss they'd shared.

"What's your answer, Abby?" Mitch asked, his voice vibrating with suppressed emotion.

Abby bit down on the inner softness of her mouth, welcoming the pain that distracted her for a few precious moments from the need racing through her. Her heart and practically every part of her was urging her to say yes, to agree to Mitch's strange proposal, to seize with both hands what he was offering.

But tempting as it was, sanity prevailed. Taking a ragged breath, she broke free of the embrace, all the while fighting to steady the thunderous roar of her blood as it sped through her veins, wreaking havoc along the way.

Bravely she met his gaze. "Mitch, I don't—" she began, then stumbled to a halt when an emotion she couldn't decipher, an emotion he quickly controlled, flickered in the silvery blue depths of his eyes.

"Think about it," he quickly cut in, managing to keep the panic out of his voice. She'd been about to refuse, he'd seen it in her eyes, seen, too, the look of anguish that had flitted across her face moments ago, and wondered at the cause of it. "Look…maybe it is a bit extreme, but if you'd just think about it for a while, think about what it would mean to Toby—" Mitch broke off. He knew it wasn't fair to try to use emotional blackmail, but he was convinced that if she gave his suggestion more thought, she would see that marriage was the only viable solution.

"I really—"

"Please. Think about it," Mitch interrupted again.

Abby noted the lines of strain on his face and saw the plea in his eyes, a plea she found she couldn't ignore. "All right. I'll think about it," she said.

Chapter Eleven

"Mom? Are you ready?" Toby asked as he pushed open the door to his mother's bedroom. "Mitch says it's time for you guys to leave."

"Is it?" Abby replied, glancing quickly at the watch on her wrist. A shiver chased down her spine that had everything to do with nerves and the fact that she was spending the evening in Mitch's company, and nothing whatsoever to do with the winter temperature outside.

"Wow! You look really pretty, Mom," Toby said, his eyes, so like his father's, studying her intently.

"Thank you, darling," Abby replied, unsure whether to laugh or cry at the surprised expression she could see on her son's face. But Toby hadn't seen her dressed up for an evening out before. In fact, Abby couldn't recall the last time she'd gone out to a restaurant or to a movie, or anywhere, for that matter.

Glancing at her reflection in the mirror once more, Abby wished she didn't feel so self-conscious about wearing the scoop-necked black dress. It fitted her well, perhaps too well, Abby thought as she tugged at the hem in an attempt to pull the material down over her knees.

She'd unearthed the black-and-gold shawl that had belonged to her mother and pinned it to the right side of her dress with an old antique gold brooch in the shape of a Gordian knot that was her favorite piece of jewelry. The shawl, made of an expensive lace, came complete with a long fringe that just kissed the hem of her dress.

After several frustrating and unsuccessful attempts to twist her hair into a chignon at the base of her neck, she'd decided to leave it hanging loose about her shoulders. She'd applied a minimum of makeup: a hint of blusher to add color to her cheeks, a trace of eyeliner and mascara to lightly accent her eyes and a touch of bloodred lipstick to give her the boost of confidence she so sorely needed.

Throughout the week she'd been alternating between looking forward to seeing Kit, Nathan and Joyce Alexander again and wishing that Nathan would call to say the dinner was canceled because his wife had gone into labor.

"Come on, Mom. Mitch is waiting." Toby turned and scampered from the room.

Retrieving her black evening purse from the top of the dressing table and the bag containing her high-heeled shoes, Abby drew a deep, steadying breath and sent up a silent prayer that she would somehow get through the evening ahead.

By the time she'd reached the top of the stairs, Toby was already at the bottom. "See, I told you. Here she is," she heard her son announce to the man standing next to him.

Mitch followed his son's gaze to the woman at the top of the stairs. His breath locked in his throat at the sight of Abby wearing a black dress that clung to her generous curves like a limpet to a rock, while golden specks on her shawl shimmered under the lights, creating a rippling effect that was incredibly sensual.

There was a quick, surprising tremor around his heart as he watched her descend, and an emotion he'd never felt before, an emotion he didn't recognize, slowly began to unfurl inside him like the wings of a brand-new butterfly emerging from its cocoon.

His mouth felt dry, there was a dizziness in his head, and his knees felt strangely weak, all symptoms reminiscent of

how he'd felt seconds after he'd had a knife thrust into him.
But there was no knife, no assailant, only the most beautiful woman he'd ever laid eyes on.

"Abby! Aren't you a sight for sore eyes." The comment
came from Tom, who'd wheeled himself into the foyer.

"Thank you. I think," Abby said, managing a fleeting
smile as she came to a halt at the foot of the stairs. Careful
to avoid Mitch's gaze, she crossed to the closet and slid her
feet into her winter boots, conscious all the while of Mitch
staring at her, almost as if he'd never seen her before.

"What do you say, son?" Tom turned to Mitch.
"Doesn't she look beautiful?"

Mitch had to swallow several times to alleviate the dryness in his throat. Dragging his eyes away from Abby, he
met his father's humor-filled gaze. "Quite beautiful,"
Mitch acknowledged in a voice he wasn't sure even belonged to him.

"Abby, my dear, you make me wish I was thirty years
younger," Tom said in a teasing tone.

On any other occasion Mitch might have found it amusing to watch his father flirt with Abby, but instead another
emotion, one he recognized as jealousy, began to writhe like
an angry serpent inside him.

Mitch shook his head, as if in denial, and cleared his
throat. "We'd better be going. We don't want to be late,"
he said. "Here, let me help you with that."

As he moved to take Abby's coat, Mitch felt his pulse
kick into high gear when the sweet scent of lilacs suddenly
bombarded his senses. It was all Mitch could do not to bury
his face in the silky softness of her hair and kiss the sensitive cord of her neck.

"Give my best to Joyce and to Kit and Nathan," Tom
said.

Mitch drew a ragged breath as he took a step back. "We
will," he replied, fighting to stem the need rushing through
him and wishing fervently that he was spending the evening alone with Abby, instead of sharing her with friends
and neighbors.

"Bye, Mom," Toby said.

"Be good...both of you," Abby said with a shaky smile at Tom and Toby, all the while wondering if she'd imagined the way Mitch's hands had lingered on her shoulders a moment ago, causing her heart to skip several beats.

Outside, the sun had long since set, and the temperature was slowly dropping. Even through the thickness of her coat Abby was aware of Mitch's hand at her elbow as they crossed the snow-covered ground to the truck.

"Thank you," she murmured as Mitch opened the passenger door for her. Abby buckled her seat belt and waited for Mitch to join her, ignoring the tiny tremors of excitement vibrating through her.

In the shadowed darkness of the truck's interior Abby glanced surreptitiously at the man beside her as he buckled his seat belt and started the engine. Beneath his outer coat Mitch wore a pair of black slacks, a white cotton shirt with a thin gray stripe and a gray-and-red patterned tie. His double-breasted jacket served to accentuate the breadth of his shoulders and Abby felt her stomach muscles tighten in a response that was all too familiar.

Hair black as night, thick and unruly, yet silky to the touch; dark eyebrows hooding eyes that glinted like chips of blue ice or flared with passion, dark and mysterious. An aquiline nose and a jaw with only a hint of stubble, making her fingers itch to explore its masculine texture.

And his mouth...full and sensual, a perfect shape, a perfect fit. She shuddered, remembering the last kiss they'd shared, the latent power, the urgency and the driving need, a need she'd eagerly matched with her own.

That was the night Mitch had asked her to think about his proposal, or rather his solution. And for the past four days Abby had done little else.

There was no question that Toby would be thrilled to learn that Mitch was his real father, and Abby felt sure Tom would welcome the news that Toby was his grandchild. But seven years ago she'd accepted Cal's marriage proposal for all the wrong reasons and landed herself in a worse mess, and she was determined not to make the same mistake twice.

But Abby's heart kept insisting that this time it was different, that this time she was deeply and irrevocably in love with the man who'd asked her to marry him, only she couldn't seem to get beyond the fact that, like Cal, Mitch also regarded marriage as a solution, a means to an end.

Much as she loved Mitch, needed him, wanted him, Abby continually came back to the same question. Could she be truly happy married to a man who didn't love her?

A marriage without love, without a deep and binding commitment from both parties, was a marriage doomed to fail. Hadn't she already learned that lesson? How long would it be before Mitch began to miss the excitement and challenge of his job? How long before he grew to resent the fact that he'd given up his career for her? How long before their marriage started to crumble?

"Looks like it might snow again tonight." Mitch's deep, resonant voice cut through Abby's wayward thoughts, bringing her out of her reverie.

Glancing at the sky, Abby saw the clouds gathering anew. "Have you listened to a weather forecast lately?" she asked.

"The weather report on the radio said something about intermittent snow flurries for tonight and tomorrow," Mitch replied.

"We should have asked Tom whether his bunion had been acting up," Abby commented.

The sound of Mitch's low rumble of laughter sent a shiver of awareness skimming across her nerve endings.

"I can't believe the change that's come over my father this past week," Mitch said. "He's approved of the changes I've made at the store. And he even supports the idea of putting in a computer system to keep better track of the stock."

Abby caught the flash of Mitch's white teeth in the dimness of the cab. "That's great," she said. Tom was indeed improving by leaps and bounds, and Abby knew it was only a matter of time before he would no longer need the services of a live-in nurse and housekeeper.

"Ah...here's the turnoff," Mitch said as he left the highway and headed down the road leading to the Alexander Winery.

"Oh, don't the Christmas lights look lovely?" Abby said as the house came into view.

"You could almost picture Santa's sleigh landing on the rooftop," Mitch said. "Which reminds me. Has Toby's bike come in yet? There's only a few more days left till Christmas."

"Yes, it has," Abby replied. "Jack Lucas from the bike shop called yesterday to tell me it's in."

"Would you like me to pick it up and bring it home tomorrow?" Mitch asked as he brought the truck to a halt behind several other vehicles parked in the driveway. "I can hide it in the woodshed under a tarpaulin."

"Thanks, Mitch. I'd appreciate that," Abby said.

"No problem," came the prompt reply. "So, is Santa bringing everything on Toby's list?" he asked as he turned off the engine.

Abby sighed and shook her head. "Not everything, I'm afraid."

"Oh..." Mitch sounded surprised. "Didn't you do your last-minute shopping the other day?" he asked, referring to the afternoon Abby had driven into town to stock up on groceries. While in town she'd taken the opportunity to shop for a few stocking stuffers for Toby, as well as a small gift each for Tom and Mitch. She'd also paid a quick trip to her basement apartment to collect a pair of black silk stockings and her high-heeled shoes.

"Yes, I did," Abby confirmed. "But there's something on Toby's list he's been a bit secretive about. I've tried to coax it out of him, but so far I haven't had any luck."

Mitch frowned, making no comment. As he climbed out of the truck and came around to open the passenger door for Abby, his thoughts drifted back to the letter he'd seen on the kitchen table, the letter Toby had been writing to Santa. Suddenly Mitch recalled the item on Toby's list that had puzzled him at the time. Could that be the secret Toby was reluctant to share?

All at once the sound of dogs barking cut through the quiet night air, and moments later the front door of the Spanish-style house opened.

"Hello, there!" Nathan called from the doorway. "I thought I heard a vehicle. Glad you could make it. Come on in," he invited when they reached him. "You remember Mark." He nodded to the boy, wearing pajamas and slippers, sitting at the foot of the stairs.

"Hello, Mark." Mitch and Abby spoke in unison.

"Hi," Mark replied.

"Let me take your coat," said Nathan to Abby.

"Thank you," Abby responded. "I see you're ready for bed, Mark," she went on after she'd changed out of her boots and into her shoes.

"Mark's actually conducting a survey," Nathan told them, a twinkle of humor in his eyes.

"A survey?" Mitch repeated. "Is it for school?" he asked as he drew alongside Abby.

"No," Mark said. "Kit said it works like magic."

Abby frowned. "What works like magic?" she asked.

"The mistletoe," Mark said, pointing above their heads. "Kit says whenever a couple stands under the mistletoe they just can't resist . . . kissing, that is." He scrunched his nose in obvious distaste.

Abby glanced up at the sprig of mistletoe suspended from the light fixture directly above them. Her eyes instantly flew to meet Mitch's in time to see an emotion flare in their depths, an emotion he quickly controlled.

"You know, Kit's right," Mitch said, a hint of amusement in his voice. "There's definitely something magical about mistletoe," he added moments before his mouth came down to capture Abby's in a kiss that was achingly tender and all too brief.

"Three couples, three kisses. Survey's over, son," Nathan said with a soft chuckle. "Say good-night."

Mark gave a beleaguered sigh. "Good night," he said as he turned and made his way upstairs.

"Sorry about that," Nathan said. "Kit loves to tease him." He ushered Abby and Mitch into the living room.

Abby made no reply. Her lips still tingled from the contact with Mitch, and it was all she could do to concentrate on the names and faces as Nathan introduced the other guests: Carmen and Bruce McGregor, David and Jean Johnstone, and Jim Donald, a friend of Joyce's.

"Mitch, Abby. It's so nice to see you both again," Kit said, squeezing first Abby's hand then Mitch's. "How's your father?" she asked Mitch.

"Back on his feet and doing well," Mitch was happy to report.

"Kit, you look absolutely radiant," Abby said, noting the glow of happiness in Kit's eyes. "But how are you feeling? Your due date's less than a week away now."

"I feel wonderful, though I've had a bit of a backache all day today," Kit told them. "But that's par for the course. I think we'll both be glad when this little bundle of joy decides it's time to venture out into the big world. Won't we, darling?"

Nathan, who'd been standing with his arm around his wife, smiled adoringly into Kit's upturned face. Abby watched the look that passed between husband and wife and felt a sharp stab of envy for the love they so obviously shared.

"We will indeed, my love," Nathan responded before dropping a brief kiss on his wife's lips. "Enough about babies. Abby, can I get you something?"

"I've heard great things about your winery," Abby answered. "I'd really like to try a glass of your wine."

Nathan smiled. "Thank you," he acknowledged. "I think I can manage to rustle up a bottle of our best. Would you prefer red or white?"

"White, please," she replied.

"Mitch? What can I interest you in?" Nathan asked.

"I've grown very fond of your cabernet," Mitch said.

"Great choice," Nathan returned. "Excuse me. I'll be right back," he added before withdrawing.

When Nathan returned to the living room a short time later, Abby was seated on a love seat chatting to Joyce Alexander, while Mitch had strolled over to the fireplace to talk to one of the other couples.

For Abby the evening was one she knew she'd remember for a long time. Kit led her guests into the dining room where the table was set with a beautiful English bone china dinner service, on a linen tablecloth decorated with sprigs of holly.

Nathan was in charge of the seating arrangements and Abby found herself seated to the left of her host, while Mitch sat next to Kit at the opposite end of the table.

The first course, a bowl of steaming tomato basil soup, was simply a taste sensation, and the main course, comprising a stuffed Cornish game hen cooked in an orange glaze, accompanied by asparagus spears, baby carrots and roast potatoes, was equally delicious.

Throughout dinner conversation flowed back and forth amid the guests, and several animated discussions ensued on various topics. Abby found her gaze continually straying to Mitch at the other end of the table, and each time her heart would skip a beat as their glances collided. It was almost as if he knew instinctively she was looking at him, and this thought sent a shiver of awareness chasing down her spine.

Mitch barely tasted the food on his plate so absorbed was he in keeping an eye on Abby. He was annoyed at the fact that they'd been placed at opposite ends of the dinner table, but there was little he could do about it.

He managed for the most part to contribute to the conversation going on around him, but found his attention constantly drawn toward Abby. Each time he heard the soft sound of her laughter, each time he glimpsed her smile, he felt his body tense.

To his surprise he realized that the emotion churning inside him once again was jealousy. He was jealous of the fact that Abby was laughing and smiling at someone else.

By the time dessert was served, Mitch was beginning to feel like a tiger trapped in a cage, and he began to wonder if the meal would ever end.

"Don't you agree, Mitch?"

The question came from Kit and Mitch, hiding his annoyance, turned his attention to his hostess. "I'm sorry Kit. What did you say? You'll have to excuse me. I'm afraid

I'm a little distracted tonight," he confessed, feeling a trifle guilty.

"A *little* distracted," Kit repeated with a teasing smile. She leaned closer as if to make sure no one but Mitch would hear her. "I'd say you've got it pretty bad," she murmured.

Mitch frowned, pushing his half-eaten dessert away. "I'm sorry? I don't think I understand," he said politely, finding it increasingly difficult to keep his mind on what Kit was saying. The sweet sound of Abby's laughter caught his attention once more and like a magnet his gaze began to drift in her direction.

"Your distraction is looking rather lovely tonight," Kit said in a low voice.

"Yes, she is," Mitch agreed, then swung his eyes back to Kit, who was grinning mischievously.

"Gotcha!" Kit declared.

Mitch sighed and reached for his wineglass. "Touché," he said before taking a sip.

"Does Abby know?" Kit asked.

"Know what?" Mitch countered, twisting the stem of the wineglass.

Kit laughed softly. "That you're in love with her, of course," she said matter-of-factly before rising slowly from her chair.

Mitch stared in stunned surprise at his hostess. He opened his mouth to reject her suggestion, to tell Kit she was mistaken, but the words never made it to his lips as the truth hit him like a thunderbolt.

"Oh, dear," said Kit, suddenly sounding a little breathless. "Nathan, darling." Kit's voice, urgent and a little alarmed now, cut through the conversation at the table.

Abby glanced at her hostess, instantly seeing the look of pain and distress on Kit's face. Jumping to her feet, Abby hurried to Kit's side and was joined instantly by Nathan as well as Dr. McGregor.

"Kit? Darling? Is it the baby? Is it time?" Nathan asked, his face etched with concern.

"I believe it is," his wife replied and followed her words with a fresh grimace of pain. "The little rascal has decided that tonight's the night to make a grand entrance." Kit managed a smile.

Less than five minutes later Nathan and Kit were on their way to the Peachville hospital. Once the excitement had died down, everyone pitched in to help Joyce clear away the dishes, lingering for a while over the coffee she insisted on serving.

The fact that the host and hostess had gone, however, put a damper on the evening's festivities and it wasn't long before the party began to break up. Abby and Mitch were the last to leave and after extracting a promise from Joyce that she would call and let them know the outcome, they climbed into the truck for the journey home.

Mitch was silent as they made their way back to the highway, his thoughts, as they had been for most of the night, on the woman beside him. He was still trying to come to terms with the startling discovery he'd made moments before Kit and Nathan's baby had interrupted the evening's proceedings.

In the dim interior of the cab Mitch threw Abby a fleeting glance, wondering whether or not she'd made a decision regarding his marriage proposal. He cringed inwardly now as he recalled the cold, rather impersonal and abrupt way he'd presented his proposal, making it sound like a solution to a problem.

But at the time his primary concern had been to become a part of Toby's life, with marriage the best and most viable option, at least from his point of view. Mitch's heart sank as he realized with a tremendous feeling of guilt that ever since he'd learned the news about Toby, he'd been selfishly thinking of himself.

He hadn't considered Abby's feelings or the fact that she could easily have lied to him and denied that Toby was his son. But she'd told him the truth, bravely facing down his skepticism with a poise and self-possession he couldn't help but admire.

On the other hand, he'd behaved abominably, intent on his own problems, too wrapped up with his feelings of discontentment and dissatisfaction, feelings that had been ultimately responsible for bringing him home in search of an answer to the question: where was he going with his life?

When he'd joined the police force he'd had those youthful aspirations every young cop harbors, to rid the world of at least some of the bad guys, to make a difference. And he'd succeeded, at least at first, and had been proud of the fact that he'd been able to put a few of the worst criminals behind bars.

But for the past year the war against crime had become increasingly difficult, the battles more dangerous and the victories fewer and farther between. His recent brush with a knife-wielding punk had been the final straw, forcing him to face the fact that he had become a liability to his fellow agents, a liability they could well do without.

It was as he'd lain in the hospital bed in Toronto, feeling drained and empty, that his thoughts had turned to his father, to the only family he had left. The urge to take a pilgrimage home had been strong indeed and, never one to disregard his instincts, he'd heeded the call.

Seeing Abby again had stirred old memories and powerful emotions, emotions he hadn't bothered to analyze or try to understand. But he'd never been in love before, never experienced these overwhelming yet tender, compelling yet captivating emotions that left him weak with longing and bound to her forever.

He knew now that he loved this woman, that this was where he wanted to be, here with Abby and their son, for better, for worse, for always. He'd come home to make peace with his father and find inner peace for himself and he'd found so much more.

His future happiness lay in Abby's hands and suddenly he couldn't wait any longer—he needed to know her answer now. Turning the wheel, he pulled the truck off the road and into a snow-covered bank before bringing it to a halt.

"Is something wrong?" Abby asked, jolted by Mitch's sudden and unexpected action.

"Nothing's wrong," Mitch responded as he released his seat belt and angled his body to face her. "I thought this was as good a time as any to find out if you've made a decision.''

Abby's heart leapt into her throat. "You want to know now?'' she asked, thinking it was ironic that ever since they'd left the Alexander Winery she'd been trying to convince herself that marriage to Mitch might work after all.

Throughout the evening she'd watched the way Kit had looked at Nathan, noticed the small intimate glances, seen the secret smiles they'd shared and found herself wishing and dreaming and hoping for a love like theirs.

For the past five minutes she'd been telling herself that if she loved Mitch enough, maybe one day he would learn to love her... and maybe cows would fly.

"Yes, I want to know now." Mitch's voice, crisp and precise, cut through her wandering thoughts and bravely she lifted her eyes to his.

In the shadowed darkness of the truck's interior she couldn't see his face, or the expression in his pale blue eyes, but she could feel the tension emanating from him and wondered at its cause.

Abby drew a steadying breath. "I'm sorry, Mitch, but I can't marry you," she said quietly and simply.

Mitch shut his eyes against the pain wrenching at his heart. It was the answer he'd expected, but that didn't make the pain any easier to bear. He had to force the breath from his lungs and clench his teeth to stop the moan of anguish building inside him from escaping.

They sat in silence for several long moments before Mitch voiced the question he wasn't altogether sure he wanted to know the answer to.

"Why?"

Abby swallowed the lump in her throat and wished, for the second time in as many minutes, that she could see Mitch's face and perhaps gauge his feelings.

"Because—" She stopped and tried again. "Because—" She broke off. "What does it matter?" she challenged, surprised to discover that she was close to tears.

"Please, Abby. I need to know. It matters to me," Mitch said softly, insistently.

Abby sighed. "Marriage isn't a solution," she said at last. "I married Cal because he told me it was the best solution, that I'd be doing the right thing for my baby and for me. But he was wrong.

"Now you're asking me to marry you for the same reason, because it's the best solution, for you...for Toby. But I won't...I won't marry without love, because a marriage without love isn't a marriage at all. Believe me. I know. I've been there." Out of breath, she came to a halt.

"Are you saying you didn't love Roberts?" His voice sounded rough and strained.

"No, I didn't love Cal," she responded in a whisper.

"Then why did you marry him?" Mitch wanted to know.

"Because I was pregnant and frightened and alone. Because Cal was very persuasive and very convincing. Because he was good at manipulating...because I was a fool. Take your pick," Abby told him wryly, wishing as she had numerous times over the years that she'd sought help elsewhere instead of turning to Cal. "I know you only want Toby," she hurried on. "And I'm willing to give you access to your son anytime, anywhere. But don't you see? Marriage is a commitment two people make because they love each other, not because it's the best solution."

The silence that followed her words was electrifying. Mitch had to clear his throat several times before he could speak.

"You're wrong about me only wanting Toby," Mitch said, his voice husky with emotion. "Because I want you, too, Abby. I've just been too blind and stupid to realize it, until tonight."

Abby's heart kicked against her ribs in startled reaction. Had he really said that he wanted her? Could she believe him? She peered into the shadows, needing desparately to see his face.

"If this is a trick to change my mind, it won't work," she told him, trying to ignore the small bubble of hope nudging its way to the surface.

"It isn't a trick," Mitch said, hurt by her response but understanding her reaction all the same. Moving out of the shadows, he leaned toward her and, bringing his hands up to gently capture her face, he bravely threw caution to the wind. "I'm in love with you, Abby. I've been in love with you since the night we made love, but I wasn't ready or willing to admit it then. Not to myself, not to you. But I am now."

Abby's lungs forgot how to function and her heart shuddered to a halt at the expression she could see in the depths of Mitch's eyes. So naked and vulnerable was the look in his eyes, so honest and pure the emotion, she felt as if he was handing her his heart and soul.

Slowly, agonizingly she released the breath trapped in her lungs, and as her heart began to pick up speed once more she managed to find her voice. "Am I dreaming? Did you just tell me you loved me?" Abby asked in a throaty whisper.

"You're not dreaming, Abby. Let me prove it to you," Mitch said a split second before he closed the gap between them.

His kiss was as soft and gentle as a raindrop in summer, slipping under her guard and into her heart before she had time to react. His mouth worshiped and revered, dispelling all the doubts she harbored, making them vanish like morning mist in the warmth of the sunshine.

His lips hovered at the corner of her mouth before skimming along her jaw to touch the pulse throbbing erratically just below her ear. His teeth playfully nipped her earlobe before he feathered soft, wet kisses at her temple and over her eyelids until she thought she might die from the wonder of it.

With his mouth, Mitch accomplished what mere words would never have achieved, and as he continued his tender assault, making another delicate foray across her cheek to tantalizingly tease the corner of her lips, Abby's heart silently accepted and acknowledged the love he was so skillfully declaring.

On a low moan of surrender Abby murmured his name, and it took every vestige of self-control to ignore her plea. But Mitch had something important to say first, something she deserved to hear.

Withdrawing a scant inch away, he drew a ragged breath. "I know I wasn't there for you seven years ago when you needed me, Abby, but you must believe me when I say that I'll never knowingly let you or Toby down again—" He broke off, suddenly blinking back tears and fighting for control. "I love you and I'm asking you to be my wife, my lover, my friend. I want to try to make it up to you and to Toby. And if I'm lucky, maybe one day you'll be able to forgive me. Maybe one day you'll be able to love me half as much as I love you."

"Oh, Mitch," Abby said huskily, immeasurably moved by what he'd just said. "Don't you know that there's never been anyone but you? I love you. I've always loved you." Her voice vibrated with suppressed emotion.

Stunned, Mitch gazed into eyes brimming with truth as well as tears. "Would you please repeat that," he said, knowing he didn't deserve this but wanting to be sure, needing to be sure.

Abby smiled. "I love you. I love you. I love—"

Although he doubted he'd ever grow tired of hearing her say those words, Mitch silenced her with a kiss that sent their world spinning out of control, transporting them to a place only lovers go, only lovers know.

It was some time before they resurfaced. Mitch reluctantly broke the kiss, silently cursing the smallness of the truck's cab and chastising himself for not waiting until they'd reached the relative comfort of home before declaring his love.

But he wasn't ready yet to let her go, and so he held Abby tightly against his heart, thrilling at the knowledge that theirs would be a happy ending. And as he waited for his heartbeat to slow to a more normal rate, he sent up a silent prayer of thanks to the powers that be for sending him a woman like Abby, a woman willing to forgive, a woman with so much love in her heart.

"Mitch?"

"Hmm," he responded.

Abby pulled away, but only far enough to be able to see his face. "Toby and I can move back to Vancouver with you, if that's what you want," she told him. "I won't let you throw away your career because of us. I don't want you to ever have regrets—"

Mitch put a finger to her lips, wondering what he'd done to deserve such a loving and generous woman. "My decision to quit has nothing to do with you," he said. "It's been in the cards for a while. That part of my life is over. I'm quitting because I want to."

Although Abby heard the ring of truth in his voice, she wasn't altogether convinced. "But are you sure staying here in Peachville and working at the market is what you want?" she asked.

"To tell you the truth, I'm surprised at how much I am enjoying it," Mitch replied. "And I'm beginning to understand why my father loves it, and after all I've put him through, well, I think I owe it to him to keep the family tradition going. And who knows, maybe one day my son will take over from me."

"I still can't believe this is happening," Abby said with a sigh as she snuggled against his neck, raining soft kisses on the strong column of his throat. "I can't wait to tell Toby. He'll be over the moon."

"Would you mind if we waited till Christmas morning to tell him?" Mitch asked, recalling Toby's letter to Santa, the letter where he'd asked for his *real father*.

"It's a wonderful idea," Abby said. "But why?"

"That way Toby will get everything on his list," he told her, smiling to himself.

"Everything?" Abby repeated with a frown. "I don't understand...."

"You will," Mitch announced, and before she could say more he silenced her the best way he knew how.

* * * * *

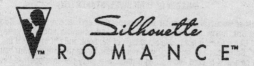

COMING NEXT MONTH

MILLION DOLLAR SWEEPSTAKES (III)

No purchase necessary. To enter the sweepstakes and receive the Free Books and Surprise Gift, follow the directions published and complete and mail your "Win A Fortune" Game Card. If not taking advantage of the book and gift offer or if the "Win A Fortune" Game Card is missing, you may enter by hand-printing your name and address on a 3" X 5" card and mailing it (limit: one entry per envelope) via First Class Mail to: Million Dollar Sweepstakes (III) "Win A Fortune" Game, P.O. Box 1867, Buffalo, NY 14269-1867, or Million Dollar Sweepstakes (III) "Win A Fortune" Game, P.O. Box 609, Fort Erie, Ontario L2A 5X3. When your entry is received, you will be assigned sweepstakes numbers. To be eligible entries must be received no later than March 31, 1996. No liability is assumed for printing errors or lost, late or misdirected entries. Odds of winning are determined by the number of eligible entries distributed and received.

Sweepstakes open to residents of the U.S. (except Puerto Rico), Canada, Europe and Taiwan who are 18 years of age or older. All applicable laws and regulations apply. Sweepstakes offer void wherever prohibited by law. Values of all prizes are in U.S. currency. This sweepstakes is presented by Torstar Corp., its subsidiaries and affiliates, in conjunction with book, merchandise and/or product offerings. For a copy of the official rules governing this sweepstakes offer, send a self-addressed, stamped envelope (WA residents need not affix return postage) to: MILLION DOLLAR SWEEPSTAKES (III) Rules, P.O. Box 4573, Blair, NE 68009, USA.

SWP-S1295

Silhouette

SPECIAL EDITION™®

Holiday Elopements

New Year's Resolution: Don't fall in love!

Little Amy Walsh wanted a daddy. And she had picked out single dad Travis Keegan as the perfect match for her widowed mom, Veronica—two people who wanted no part of romance in the coming year. But that was *before* Amy's relentless matchmaking efforts....

Don't miss
NEW YEAR'S DADDY
by Lisa Jackson
(SE #1004, January)

It's a HOLIDAY ELOPEMENT—the season of loving gets an added boost with a wedding. Catch the holiday spirit and the bouquet! Only from Silhouette Special Edition!

HAPPY HOLIDAYS!

Silhouette Romance celebrates the holidays with
six heartwarming stories of the greatest gift of all—
love that lasts a lifetime!

#1120 *Father by Marriage*
by Suzanne Carey

#1121 *The Merry Matchmakers*
by Helen R. Myers

#1122 *It Must Have Been the Mistletoe*
by Moyra Tarling

#1123 *Jingle Bell Bride*
by Kate Thomas

#1124 *Cody's Christmas Wish*
by Sally Carleen

#1125 *The Cowboy and the Christmas Tree*
by DeAnna Talcott

COMING IN DECEMBER FROM

**HE'S NOT JUST A MAN,
HE'S ONE OF OUR**

A FATHER'S VOW
Elizabeth August

From the moment single dad Lucas Carver saw Felicity Burrow, he knew she was special. His little boy knew it too—young Mark's first words were "Make Felicity my mom!" Felicity touched Lucas's heart in ways he'd never dreamed possible, and now Lucas was determined to win her!

Fall in love with our Fabulous Fathers!

Coming in January, only from

Silhouette
R O M A N C E™

INTRODUCING...  WINNER'S CIRCLE

A collection of award-winning books by award-winning authors! From Harlequin and Silhouette.

Falling Angel
by Anne Stuart

WINNER OF THE RITA AWARD
FOR BEST ROMANCE!

Falling Angel by Anne Stuart is a RITA Award winner, voted Best Romance. A truly wonderful story, *Falling Angel* will transport you into a world of hidden identities, second chances and the magic of falling in love.

"Ms. Stuart's talent shines like the brightest of stars, making it very obvious that her ultimate destiny is to be the next romance author at the top of the best-seller charts."
—*Affaire de Coeur*

A heartwarming story for the holidays. You won't want to miss award-winning *Falling Angel,* available this January wherever Harlequin and Silhouette books are sold.

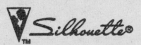